8

PW

Indulge in some perfect romance from the incomparable

PENNY JORDAN

The all new Penny Jordan large print collection gives you your favourite glamorous Penny Jordan stories in easier-to-read print.

Penny Jordan has been writing for more than twenty-five years and has an outstanding record: over 165 novels published including the phenomenally successful A PERFECT FAMILY, TO LOVE, HONOUR AND BETRAY, THE PERFECT SINNER and POWER PLAY which hit *The Sunday Times* and *New York Times* bestseller lists. She says she hopes to go on writing until she has passed the 200 mark, and maybe even the 250 mark.

Penny is a member and supporter of both the Romantic Novelists' Association and the Romance Writers of America—two organisations dedicated to providing support for both published and yet-to-be published authors.

PERFECT MARRIAGE MATERIAL

Penny Jordan

First published in Great Britain 1997
Large Print Edition 2011
Harlequin Mills & Boon Limited,
Eton House, 18-24 Paradise Road,
Richmond, Surrey TW9 1SR

ISBN: 978 0 263 22314 9

Harlequin Mills & Boon policy is to use papers that are natural, renewable and recyclable products and made from wood grown in sustainable forests. The logging and manufacturing process conform to the legal environmental regulations of the country of origin.

Printed and bound in Great Britain
by CPI Antony Rowe, Chippenham, Wiltshire

CHAPTER ONE

TULLAH reached tiredly for the receiver as the telephone started to ring. She had just walked into her flat. Despite the fact that the company she worked for was cutting back on both taking on and promoting staff, the amount of work passing over her desk seemed to increase every day. Officially she finished at five-thirty but tonight, just like every other night for the past six weeks or so, it had been gone nine before she actually left work. But not for much longer… Thank goodness.

"Tullah Richards," she announced softly into the receiver in the faintly husky and rather sensual voice that her friends teased her sounded far too sexy for the determined career woman she proclaimed herself to be.

"Tullah! Wonderful. I've been trying to get hold of you all day. It's still on for this weekend, isn't it?"

Tullah smiled as she recognised the voice of

Olivia. She and Olivia had worked together a few years earlier and had remained good friends even though Olivia was now married with a small daughter and living in the Cheshire countryside, whilst she had remained in London determinedly pursuing her chosen career path. But not for much longer. By an odd quirk of fate, she, too, would soon be moving to Haslewich….

"Yes, if it's still OK with you," she responded to Olivia's question.

"We're looking forward to it," Olivia assured her. "What time do you expect to arrive?"

"About five, I think. I'm supposed to be meeting the rep from the relocation people at one and we're going to go round several properties they've picked out for me."

"Properties…that sounds very grand," Olivia teased.

Tullah laughed. "I wish," she agreed. "Actually I've already told them that I shan't be able to afford anything much more expensive than a single-bedroomed flat, or preferably a small cottage, although I understand with the influx of new residents from Aarlston-Becker relocating to Haslewich, property locally is at something of a premium."

"Some of it is," Olivia agreed. "I think initially there was a feeling amongst the upper echelons of Aarlston-Becker that they'd be able to exchange their city semis for seven-bedroomed country mansions and ex-vicarages, complete with paddocks for ponies and Gertrude Jekyll-style gardens. However, the reality hasn't been quite like that. Property *is* cheaper here, but… There are some very pretty little houses in Haslewich itself. Great-Aunt Ruth already has four new neighbours on Church Walk where she lives and we've certainly been handling a big increase in conveyances.

"What will happen about your London flat, by the way?"

"Oh well, I've been quite lucky there. Sarah, the girl I share with, is getting married and she and her new husband are buying me out, so at least I'm not having to hang fire waiting for a buyer, although part of the deal when Aarlston-Becker offered me the job was that they would cover all my moving costs, including any bridging loans I might need, plus making sure I got a mortgage."

"That's my girl." Olivia laughed. "I must say I'm really looking forward to your moving up here. It will be like old times. I can't believe sometimes that it's over three years since I left the company. So much has happened. Caspar and I've married and we've had Amelia, the practice has really become busy this past year and Uncle Jon and I have been talking about taking on a qualified legal assistant or even possibly a full solicitor."

"Mmm...well, you certainly did make the right decision leaving when you did," Tullah assured her darkly. "The amount of cutbacks we've been having are quite frightening."

"They'll be sorry to lose you, though," Olivia returned. "I must say I felt awfully proud of you when I heard that you'd been head-hunted to join Aarlston-Becker."

"Along with a good dozen or so other people," Tullah felt bound to point out, "and only because they'd decided to relocate to Haslewich almost at the last minute instead of going ahead with their original plans to move their European divisional headquarters to The Hague because the British incentives were so much better."

"Well, you're certainly going to be working for a first-class international organisation," Olivia told her enthusiastically. "I know how impressed my cousin Saul has been since he joined them six months ago. Like you, he, too, was head-hunted by them when they first relocated and—"

"Saul," Tullah interrupted her, an unusual sharpness entering her normally soft husky voice.

"Mmm…he's one of my cousins, well, perhaps a second or even a third on my father's side. I'm never quite sure with our tangled family history. You may not remember him although he was at the wedding and the christening, as well. Tall, dark and—"

"Handsome," Tullah supplied grittily, adding trenchantly, "So far as I can remember, Olivia, you have at least half a dozen second and third male cousins who could answer that description."

"Maybe," Olivia agreed and then her voice softened slightly as she continued, "But there's only one Saul."

"If only," Tullah muttered sourly under her breath. Then raising her voice so that Olivia could hear her, she remarked, "I do remember him—vaguely. Very dark, rather autocratic and quite the gallant, as I recall. He made a big fuss about making sure everyone knew what a good father he was, but I seem to remember it was your Aunt Jenny who actually seemed to be spending the most time looking after his children.

"I thought that his side of your family lived in Pembroke," she added disdainfully.

"They did…they do. It's just that since Uncle Hugh is virtually fully retired, he and Ann spend a good deal of their time travelling abroad. Uncle Hugh is a keen sailor and, well, to cut a long story short, Saul is divorced now and he thought it would be better for the children to grow up in an environment where they had close family ties, and in fact that was the clinching element in his taking this job with Aarlston's. Quite a coincidence, really, both of you working for their legal department but then, of course, it is a huge multinational organisation.

"There was quite a lot of local antagonism towards them when they first moved into the area. Aunt Ruth said it reminded her of when the Americans arrived during the Second World War, only *they* had the benefit of silk stockings and chocolate to ease their way into the community.

"Aunt Jenny was saying the other day that she'd heard on the local grapevine via Guy Cooke, her business partner—his widespread family *are* Haslewich, you should know. They've been here right from the word "'go'—the general consensus of opinion tends to be in favour of the influx, or at least the boost to the local economy that it brings with it."

"Mmm…well, it's good to know I shan't be facing the local eviction committee," Tullah told her ruefully.

Olivia laughed. "You? No way. It's going to be lovely having you to stay for the weekend, Tullah. I'm really looking forward to it."

"So am I," Tullah confirmed with a smile.

Once she had replaced the receiver, though, she wasn't smiling. Saul Crighton. She hadn't realised that *he* was living in Haslewich now or, even worse, working for Aarlston-Becker. She knew, of course, that Olivia had something of a soft spot for him although she couldn't understand why. By all accounts and from the gossip she had overheard at Olivia and Caspar's wedding, Saul had come very close to breaking them up, cold-bloodedly trying to persuade a then very vulnerable Olivia into having an affair with him, even though he had been married at the time.

And if that wasn't bad enough, Tullah had also overheard the same two people discussing the fact that one of Olivia's young teenage cousins, Louise, was in all likelihood also a victim of Saul's egotistical and grossly selfish need to boost his flagging self-esteem in the only way he apparently knew how—flattering and seducing young, immature and vulnerable girls into having affairs with him.

Tullah knew all about that kind of man and she knew, too, just what sort of devastation they could wreak, just what kind of hurt and self-loathing they could inflict on their victims. She *should* do. She after all…

But it was pointless harking back to the past. She had very firmly closed the door on that particular episode of her life when she had come to live and work in London. The young girl who had fallen so intensely and so damagingly in love with the married man who had cold-bloodedly fed on her naïvety and inexperience, her belief that when he said he loved her and his marriage was an empty sham, he truly meant it, no longer existed. How could she? She had been damaged beyond repair, destroyed by the trauma of discovering just how much her lover had deceived her, by learning that not only had he no intention of leaving his wife but that also, far from being the love of his life, she was actually just one in a long, long chain of affairs he had lured his victims into over the years.

If she was honest with herself, she could see now that it wasn't so much her youthful love and adoration that still festered deep down inside her, but the humiliation he had wrought, the self-hatred, the awareness of her own foolishness and gullibility.

His wife had told her wearily at the time that the only reason she had not left him was because of their children.

"*They* still need him even if I don't," she had told Tullah tiredly, and Tullah, aware humiliatingly of how much she missed her own father since her own parents' divorce, had to bite down hard on her bottom lip to prevent herself from crying like a child herself.

Over the years she had come into contact with a good many men who suffered from the same egocentric needs as the man who had hurt her so badly—shallow, vain creatures, possessed of a dangerously alluring charm that could all too easily deceive the vulnerable and naïve, and so far there was no doubt whatsoever in her mind that Saul Crighton was yet another example of the breed.

She remembered that he had asked her to dance at Olivia and Caspar's wedding, frowning down at her from his admittedly impressive height of over six feet when she had refused as tersely and abruptly as a child.

She could remember, too, watching Olivia fuss over him, explaining when she saw Tullah watching her that he had been going through a bad time and that he carried a heavy burden of responsibility.

"He and his wife...are separated," she had explained, a little uncomfortably when Tullah had made no response. Tullah had said nothing, not wanting to cause any discord between Olivia and her by informing her friend that she was not surprised. After all, she had just overheard about Saul's attempt to seduce Olivia away from Caspar.

It had been Max Crighton, another of Olivia's cousins, Jon and Jenny's elder son, who had explained the whole situation to her.

"Saul likes "em young...he's at that age," Max had told her cynically. "Mind you, he's not exactly the faithful type. No sooner had he realised that he'd lost Olivia than he started making a play for my sister Louise."

She had spent a good half an hour listening to Max explaining the intricate interfamily relationships that existed between the various members of the Crighton clan. He himself was quite obviously very much a man who liked to flirt, but Tullah had found his frank and open attempts to engage her in a subtly sensual exchange of banter far more healthy and easy to deal with than, to her mind, Saul's much more sinister and underhanded pseudo sincerity, especially when she had seen Louise, all coltish limbs and soft, trembling mouth, watching him with her heart in her eyes. No, she hadn't liked Saul Crighton a bit…not one tiny little bit.

"You're looking very thoughtful and broody," Caspar commented to his wife as he walked into the kitchen, put down the essays he had brought home to read and went over to the table where she was standing to take her in his arms and kiss her. "Mmm…that was nice."

"Mmm…very," she agreed, telling him, "I spoke to Tullah earlier. She's definitely coming up this weekend."

"Ah, now I understand. It's the thought of doing a little bit of matchmaking that's turning you all broody, isn't it, and not—"

"Well, Tullah *is* twenty-eight, just the right age

to settle down," Olivia told her husband defensively. "And she's so motherly...."

"Motherly?" Caspar gave a shout of laughter as he visualised his wife's friend. "Is this the same Tullah we're talking about? Tullah with the figure that's straight out of every man's fantasy...somewhere between Claudia Schiffer and a *Baywatch* babe? The same Tullah with those wonderful, dark gypsy eyes and curls and that gorgeous pouting mouth that makes her look so provocative and yet at the same time somehow more vulnerable and less knowing, if you know what I mean... and—"

"Caspar," Olivia warned.

"Sorry," he apologised unrepentantly. His eyes twinkled as he admitted, "Perhaps I *was* getting a trifle carried away...but you have to admit that no one would ever think she's a highly qualified lawyer. She looks as though her sex-appeal rating would be through the roof while her IQ—"

"Caspar!" Olivia warned more darkly.

"OK, OK...calm down. You know perfectly well that my taste runs to sassy blondes with flashing eyes and... All I'm trying to say," he added patiently, "is that stunning and sensual and very, very sexy Tullah may be, but motherly..."

"That's just because you're judging her on the way she looks," Olivia told him severely. "As you've just said yourself, she *is* highly qualified. She actually started working in a small professional practice, you know, but the trauma of dealing with so many divorce and custody cases got to her so much that she decided to switch to industry instead. Her own parents split up when she was in her teens, and from what she's told me about it, I suspect it had a very traumatic effect on her."

"Mmm…very probably." They exchanged long, understanding looks with one another. Caspar's own childhood had not been an easy one, passed as he had been from parent to parent, forced to take a back seat as they both remarried and produced further families, which in his mind seemed to supplant him.

Olivia's childhood, too, had not been without its problems. Her father, David, her uncle Jon's twin brother, had disappeared whilst recovering from a serious heart attack, simply discharging himself and walking out, leaving no trace of where he was going or what he intended to do and her mother…

Tania, her mother, after years of suffering from an eating disorder, was now living in the south of England. She had telephoned Olivia several weeks ago to tell her excitedly that there was a new man in her life whom she wanted her daughter to meet.

"I was thinking of how perfectly one of the Chester cousins would be for Tullah," Olivia told Caspar.

"*One* of them?" he repeated, raising his eyebrows.

"Well, there are so many to choose from," she defended herself, "and now that Luke and Bobbie are married…well, it might just give the others the impetus they need. After all, it can't be lack of financial security that's holding them back."

"You sound like one of Jane Austen's characters," Caspar teased her.

Olivia laughed again. "You mean, '"It is a truth universally acknowledged, that a single man in possession of a good fortune must be in want of a wife."' she quoted. "I was thinking more of the *emotional* need," she informed Caspar with great dignity. Now let me see… There's James and Alistair, Niall and Kit." She ticked their names off on her fingers.

"She can't marry all of them," Caspar interrupted her.

"Of course not," she agreed, giving him a scathing look. "But I am sure that *one* of them... After all, just think what she's got in common with them."

"What?" Caspar invited.

"Well, for a start, they're all members of the same profession," she told him, raising her eyes to the ceiling. "Honestly, men!" She turned to the papers she had been about to read before he came in, shaking her head.

"Livvy..." She stared at Caspar as he drew her gently to him, "Look, I know you mean well, and yes, your cousins and Tullah possibly do have something in common, but she's a high-flying professional woman of almost thirty. Don't you think if she *wanted* to settle down and have children she'd have found a partner of her own choice by now?"

Olivia bit her lip. "Are you trying to tell me that I shouldn't interfere?"

"Well..."

"I was only thinking of having a couple of dinner parties...returning invitations...that kind of thing."

"Mmm... I suppose I *should* take it as a compliment that *you* enjoy marriage and motherhood so much that you want to inflict it, er, share its pleasure, with all your friends."

"I suppose you should," she agreed. "Speaking of which...do you remember how we were talking the other night about it being time we thought about a brother or sister for Amelia?"

"What, you're not—"

"Not yet," she told him demurely. "But we really ought to—"

"Oh yes, we really ought," Caspar agreed, laughing as he turned her towards the kitchen door and the stairs that lay beyond it.

CHAPTER TWO

"SO, HAVE you seen anything locally yet that's taken your fancy?" Olivia asked Tullah eagerly when she returned from the property viewings organised by the relocation agency.

"Not really, apart from this little moppet." Tullah laughed as she broke off from cuddling Amelia, Caspar and Olivia's two-year-old daughter, to answer Olivia's question.

"Ah well, if *that's* what you fancy, it isn't a house you should be looking for, it's a man," Olivia teased her gently.

"No thanks," Tullah retorted, the smile dying out of her eyes as she handed Amelia over to her mother, her full mouth compressing firmly.

"Tullah..." Olivia began, then stopped as she saw the look she was giving her. Good friends though they had always been, Tullah was the type who held herself slightly aloof from others and whom, despite her stunningly voluptuous and sensual looks, the men in the large organisation they had both worked for had very quickly learned to treat with wary caution.

Olivia knew the reason for Tullah's wariness of the male sex and she also knew that Tullah didn't like to discuss her love life.

She knew that the only time Tullah did let her guard down with men was when she was with one she knew to be happily attached to another woman. Because she felt safe with such a man?

"So *none* of the properties was any good, then?" she asked sympathetically.

Tullah pulled a face. "Well, the modern single-bedroomed flats they showed me were affordable, but very anonymous, and the cottages were either too large or too expensive or both. There was one, though...." She paused whilst Olivia waited. "Well, it just had so many things against it, and even the agent said that it had only been included on the list at the last minute, but..."

"But..." Olivia encouraged patiently.

Tullah gave her a rueful look and admitted, "But it was quite definitely a case of love at first sight."

"Oh dear," Olivia sympathised, "as bad as that?"

"And more," Tullah agreed wryly, ticking points

off on her fingers. “It’s overpriced, on the wrong side of town for work. It needs a fortune spent on it. Possibly spraying for infestation of the wood, rewiring, new plumbing—you name it. It doesn’t even have mains drainage.”

“So what *does* it have?” Olivia asked, adding helpfully, “It must have some plus points otherwise you wouldn’t have fallen for it.”

“Oh, it does,” Tullah agreed. “The place is surrounded by farm land. There’s the most wonderful view from upstairs of the river. It has a huge garden. It’s one of a pair of semis, the other half of which is owned by a couple of elderly widowed sisters who apparently travel a lot to Australia to visit relatives. The lane leading to it doesn’t go anywhere other than to a farmhouse that you can’t even *see* from my cottage.”

“A farmhouse…” Olivia was looking intrigued and slightly excited. “Where exactly is this cottage, Tullah? It sounds—”

“It sounds horrendous, I know,” Tullah finished for her, “and certainly not the sort of thing a sane, sensible, professional woman of my age should even think about buying. Even if it were a bargain, which it most certainly isn’t, it could be months before it’s even properly habitable.”

"Well, you could always stay here," Olivia offered generously, and when Tullah shook her head, she asked, "So what did you do? Tell the agent it just wasn't feasible?"

"No," Tullah admitted with a shamefaced grin. "I made an offer...."

Both of them were still laughing when Caspar walked into the kitchen and, of course, just like a man, could not really comprehend the reason for their combined mirth even when Olivia had explained the situation to him.

"Saul rang while you were out," he told Olivia. "He's going to be a little later than planned getting here for dinner this evening, something about problems with the babysitter, but he said he'll definitely be here for eight-thirty."

"That's fine. I've invited Saul and Jon and Jenny round for dinner tonight," she explained to Tullah. "Which reminds me, your cottage—" She broke off as the young retriever dog lying in its basket in front of the Aga gave a small protesting yelp as Amelia pulled its tail, gently chiding her daughter as she went to rescue the dog. "No, Amelia, you're hurting Flossy. You have to be gentle with her."

* * *

A couple of hours later as she stood in front of the pretty Victorian cheval-glass in Olivia's best guest bedroom studying her appearance, Tullah reflected that she would much rather simply have spent the evening relaxing with Olivia and Caspar instead of having to sit down and make polite dinner-party conversation. She had met both Jon and Jenny, together with Saul before and whilst she had liked the older couple, so far as Saul was concerned...

The dress she had chosen to wear had been a sale bargain she had been coaxed into getting by her mother and sister up from Hampshire for a shopping weekend, and as she had protested at the time, she didn't think it was really her.

Lucinda, her sister, had shaken her head in her elder sisterly way and told her to stop being silly. "Of course it's you. That vanilla shade is perfect with your skin colouring and hair and the dress itself couldn't be simpler or easier to wear. If I wasn't so huge at the moment I'd be tempted to buy it myself."

"Well, you aren't going to be pregnant for ever," Tullah had countered, but Lucinda had shaken her head and groaned.

"Believe me, at this stage another three months

feels like for ever, and besides, I doubt I'm *ever* going to be slim enough to wear anything like that again—or to have the occasion to wear it."

The vanilla colour of the Ghost dress *did* suit her, Tullah was forced to admit, but she was still aware that the narrow, slender, slightly clinging effect of the silky fabric with its bias cut was not something she would ever have chosen for herself.

The dress's round neckline was discreet enough, but the way the fabric moved, the way it clung sensuously to her curves… Fortunately she had spotted a separate jacket in the same fabric, which she had also brought with her. As she slipped it on, she acknowledged that she was going to be rather hot wearing it.

Downstairs the doorbell rang.

Pulling the jacket around her, Tullah hurried to the door and went downstairs, expecting to see Jon and Jenny standing in the hallway with Olivia. She came to an abrupt halt halfway down the stairs when she realised that the first arrival was not Olivia's aunt and uncle but her cousin!

"Tullah." Olivia's eyes widened slightly and appreciatively as she saw her friend.

"No matchmaking," Caspar had told her firmly, but really…it was such a waste….

"You remember Saul, don't you?" She continued smiling from Tullah to Saul, who was standing next to her.

"Yes," Tullah agreed coolly, pretending not to see the hand Saul had extended towards her and making sure that she stood on the opposite side of Olivia from him and just out of eyeshot.

"Yes…well, Caspar's in the dining room, Saul, if you'd like a drink. You obviously managed to sort out your babysitting problem," Olivia said, smiling.

"Luckily yes," he agreed. "Since the custody case, I'm having to be a bit more careful about whom I leave them with…"

As she listened to him, Tullah was glad that neither he nor Olivia was looking at her because she knew her expression must be betraying her feelings. What kind of father exactly was Saul if it took the full weight of the legal system to compel him to ensure that his young children were left provided with a proper babysitter? One read of appalling cases where small children were left with inappropriate sitters or, in some reprehensible cases, no sitter at all, often with shocking consequences. It certainly couldn't be any kind of financial hardship that prevented Saul from paying someone qualified to look after his children.

Personally she found it quite wrong that he should choose to go out during one of his children's custody visits instead of spending time with them and she was rather surprised that Olivia had encouraged him to do so.

"I'll come and give you a hand in the kitchen," she offered, shaking her head when Olivia suggested she might like to join the men for a drink whilst they waited for Jon and Jenny to arrive. The last thing she wanted was to have to spend any more time than necessary in conversation with Saul Crighton.

"Olivia was telling me that you'll soon be joining us at Aarlston-Becker," Saul commented to Tullah, shaking his head as Caspar offered to refill his wineglass. "Better not," he told the other man. "I'm driving."

Well at least he had *some* sense of responsibility, Tullah reflected, although she didn't think much of a man who quite obviously considered his driving licence to be more important than his children.

"Yes, that's right," she agreed, answering his question and then turning to Jon, who was seated on the other side of her, to ask him if the arrival of the huge multinational locally had had much effect on their own business.

"Well, it's certainly bumped up our conveyancing work," Jon replied, smiling, "although, as you know, all of Aarlston's internal and corporate legal work is handled by its own legal department. Olivia was saying that you specialised in European law."

"Yes, that's right," Tullah agreed again between spoonfuls of Olivia's delicious home-made vichyssoise. She enjoyed cooking herself, not that it was something she got much time for.

"Tullah spent a year working in The Hague," Olivia informed her uncle, smiling at her friend. "Something else you and Saul have in common," she added to Tullah. "Saul worked there for a while. That was how he met Hillary."

"Your wife?" Tullah commented coolly to Saul.

"My ex-wife," he corrected her evenly, but he

was looking at her, Tullah noticed, in a way that said he was aware of her hostility towards him.

Aware of it, she suspected, but not particularly concerned by it. But then, why should he be? By any normal standards, Saul would be considered a very attractive and personable man, and it was plain from the way they talked to him that both Olivia and Jenny had something of a soft spot for him. He was certainly not the type of man who would ever lack female company or appreciation, but he would certainly never have *hers*, and Tullah could only admire the friendly and warm way that Caspar treated him in view of the fact that Saul had deliberately tried to break up Caspar's own relationship with Olivia.

"Aarlston's certainly sounds an excellent firm to work for from what you've told us about them, Saul," Jon intervened tactfully.

"They are," Saul confirmed, adding, "In fact, they're acknowledged as being leaders in the field of sexual equality and they were one of the first multinationals to provide not just crÈche facilities for the mothers amongst their employees, but also to introduce paternal leave on the birth of a new baby as automatic. I've certainly found them very good about the amount of time I've had to take off recently over the children, especially with the custody case."

"It always amazes me how many men seem to develop a strong paternal instinct when they're threatened with losing their children," Tullah commented grittily, darting an acid look in Saul's direction.

"Fathers can tend to take their role in their children's lives for granted," Jon agreed peaceably.

Saul said nothing but he was watching her very closely, Tullah knew, and the look in his eyes did not suggest that it was any kind of male desire or approval that was prompting his visual concentration on her.

Good! If she *had* probed beneath the arrogance of his self-confidence and found a vulnerable spot, so much the better. She could still remember the anguish her father had put them all through by insisting on his visiting rights with them—visits that more often than not were forgotten or, when remembered, turned out to be miserable afternoons spent watching television in his high-rise apartment, forbidden to disturb him whilst he worked. But then, of course, it had never been their *company* he wanted. No, what he had wanted was quite simply to deprive their mother of it and to cause as much upset in her life as he could.

Olivia started to collect their empty soup dishes, and Tullah jumped up to help her.

"There's no need..." Olivia began, but Tullah shook her head, quickly gathering up her own and Jon's dishes, and then tensing as she realised that Saul had picked his up to pass to her.

The temptation to simply ignore him was so strong that she was almost on the point of doing so and turning away when she happened to catch his eye.

The cynical comprehension she could see there was disconcerting but nowhere near as disconcerting as his easy but oh so calmly determined, "You sit down. I'll take care of these," as he neatly turned the tables on her and stood up, towering above her, or so it seemed. He deftly relieved her of the dishes she was holding and then, turning away from her, told Olivia warmly, "That soup was delicious. You'll have to give me the recipe."

"Oh, it's simple enough, really," Olivia started to assure him as they both headed for the kitchen. "Just so long as you've got a decent blender."

"Saul's really determined to give the children a

stable home background, isn't he?" Jenny commented when the couple were both out of earshot. "I really do admire him for what he's trying to do."

"Why is it that when a *man's* a single parent he gets so much more sympathy than a woman in the same situation?" Tullah asked grimly. "And Saul isn't even a full-time single parent." She fell silent as the kitchen door reopened and Saul and Olivia returned.

Tullah could see that she had surprised Jenny a little by her antagonistic remark but she was growing irritated hearing Saul given so much praise that he patently did not deserve.

"Did you get much chance to visit any of the museums while you were working in The Hague?"

"Some," Tullah responded dismissively to Saul's question. She had made up her mind not to respond to the man's conversational overtures. The longer she sat and listened to the others, the more aware she was of the high esteem in which they all, but most especially Jenny and Olivia, held Saul, and for some reason that made her all the more determined to hold on to her own antagonism towards him.

Why, after all, should a man be praised simply because he took on the responsibility of his own children for one weekend in four or whatever it was that Saul's access arrangements allowed for? Even then he apparently couldn't bring himself to spend the whole of his time with them but instead found someone else to take care of them for him so that he could come out to dinner and bask in the admiration and affection of his female relatives. Some father!

She could well remember her own father doing much the same thing, leaving them with his mother, their grandmother, on the pretext of having to see someone about business.

"Tullah...I was telling Saul in the kitchen just now about the cottage you saw this afternoon. Tullah's fallen in love with a cottage she viewed earlier today," she explained for the benefit of the others. "It's—"

"It's completely out of the question," Tullah interrupted her quickly, "and totally impractical."

"Sometimes it does us good to be impractical, to indulge ourselves in our daydreams...our fantasies," she heard Saul saying. "They *are*, after all, an important part of what makes us human."

Tullah felt a small frisson of sensation run down

her spine but when she looked at him to refute what he had said she saw that he wasn't looking at her but at Olivia…and she was quite openly smiling back at him.

Tullah's head ached. She felt tired and very much aware of the fact that she stood outside the tightly knit and obviously very close family network that bonded together the other five people seated round the table with her.

"When does Louise finish university for the year?" Saul asked Jenny apparently casually.

As Tullah stiffened with shock and disgust to hear Saul questioning Jenny so carelessly about her daughter, a girl who must be almost twenty years younger than Saul himself and whom she had heard described illuminatingly as having a very intense crush on Saul, she saw that Jenny was looking uncomfortable, as well, her glance straying to her husband before she responded quietly, "Officially not for another few months although she *did* say she might come home earlier. Apparently her lectures finish a little ahead of the official end of term."

It was obvious that Jenny was ill at ease discussing her daughter with Saul, and no wonder, given what Tullah knew about the situation between them. In fact, Tullah could only marvel at both Jenny's forbearance and Saul's breathtaking arrogance and obvious disregard for Jenny and Jon's feelings as Louise's parents.

All in all, Tullah felt relieved when the evening finally came to an end and Jon and Jenny got up to leave. Shortly afterwards, declining a nightcap, Saul, too, announced that he must go.

Caspar offered to see him out and whilst they were gone Tullah followed Olivia into the kitchen to help her clear up.

"Saul's a darling," Olivia began warmly as she started to stack the dishwasher. "I just hope... wish..." She stopped speaking as she saw Tullah's expression. "You don't like him, do you?" she asked her friend quietly.

"I'm sorry, Olivia," Tullah apologised. "But no, I don't. I *know* he's your cousin, a member of your family but..." She took a deep breath and lifted her head, forcing herself to meet Olivia's expression of shocked dismay. "He's everything I most dislike in a man, Olivia. I know that you...that you and he..." She shook her head awkwardly. "I mean, just look at the way he left his children tonight to come here. A man like that doesn't deserve to be a father. He—"

"Tullah..." she heard Olivia interrupting her in a stifled warning voice, but it was too late. Tullah followed her gaze and, turning round, saw Saul standing behind her in the open doorway, a tight, furiously angry expression on his face.

"For your information, the *only* reason I *left* my children as you so ill-informedly put it to come here tonight was because Olivia asked me—"

"Saul," Olivia intervened pleadingly, "Tullah didn't mean...she doesn't realise—"

"On the contrary, I realise all too well," Tullah objected curtly.

"I came back to check if it was still all right to leave Meg with you on Monday night," Saul asked Olivia, totally ignoring Tullah.

"Yes, of course it is. Caspar will collect her from school and bring her back here."

Saul turned to leave and then seemed to hesitate, turning to look at Tullah scathingly before saying quietly, "I hope you prove to be rather more thorough and responsible in your attitude to your work than you appear to be in your attitude to your fellow human beings," he told her coldly. "Because if not..."

"Because if not, what?" Tullah challenged him, lifting her chin. He might be above her in status in the company, but his involvement with the transatlantic side of the business meant, thankfully, that they were hardly likely to come into much contact with one another.

"I must go, Livvy," Saul said, ignoring her once more. "I promised Bobbie I'd be back before twelve. She and Luke want to spend some time with Aunt Ruth and Grant before they fly back to Boston."

"Yes, I know," Olivia returned. "I think it was wonderful the way Ruth and Grant made a prenuptial agreement to each spend six months of every year living in one another's country."

"A decision worthy of Solomon," Saul agreed with a smile. His smile disappeared as he turned back towards Tullah and gave her a small, terse nod of his head before saying curtly, "Good night."

Tullah barely waited for the door to close behind Saul's departing back before saying huskily, "Would you mind if I went up to bed, Livvy? I've got a bit of a headache and—"

"No, no, you go up," Olivia assured her. Tullah knew her antagonism towards Saul had disturbed her but still she couldn't apologise for it or take back what she had said.

* * *

An hour later as she snuggled up in bed next to Caspar, Olivia told him sleepily, "I can't understand why Tullah is so antagonistic towards Saul of all people. He really is one of the nicest men you could ever meet. Uncle Hugh used to say that it was just as well Saul decided to go into industry because, despite all his professional qualifications, he just doesn't have that aggressive hard edge you need to make it to the top as a barrister. Luke's got it, of course, and—"

"Mmm…she does seem to have taken rather a dislike to him," Caspar agreed, kissing the top of her head before adding reassuringly, "It's just as well you didn't have *him* picked out as a possible father for the children you've decided Tullah wants to have." He chuckled at the thought.

"Saul and Tullah… No, that would never work," Olivia declared, laughing.

"Daddy…"

"Mmm…" Saul responded, bending down to tuck a stray curl off his younger daughter's face. She had been crying in her sleep in the grip of one of the bad nightmares she had started having whilst she was staying in America with her mother and Hillary's second husband. Having woken her gently from it and calmed her down, Saul watched her tenderly in the light from the small child's lamp as he waited for her to go back to finish whatever it was she wanted to say to him.

"You won't ever go away and leave us, will you?"

Somehow he managed to resist the impulse to snatch her up out of her small bed and hold her close.

"Well, sometimes I *do* have to go away on business," he responded calmly and matter-of-factly, "and sometimes you go away, too, when you leave to stay with Mummy, but I promise you I won't ever go away from you for very long, poppet."

"Do I really have to go and stay with Mummy even if I don't want to?"

Saul's heart sank.

He had tried his best to explain to the children that they were Hillary's children as well as his and that she loved them and wanted them with her. The older two, Robert and Jemima, had understood even though they had both forcefully expressed their desire to stay with him. With Meg, however, it was proving much harder to explain that it was not just a legal requirement that her mother had access to her, but also his own conviction that at some stage in their lives all three children were going to want to have contact with their mother and that if he acceded to their desire now not to have to visit her, then not only would he be guilty of depriving them of an emotional bond he believed they needed to have, but ultimately there could possibly come a time when they would blame him as an adult and their father for allowing them to make a decision they were at present too immature emotionally to make. And it was for that reason, for *their* sakes, that he had been at such pains to keep his divorce from Hillary and the subsequent custody case as unacrimonious as possible.

As it was, it would be a long time before he forgot the telephone call he had received from Hillary three months ago, hysterically demanding that he fly over to America immediately and collect the children because they were destroying her relationship with her new husband, who had demanded that she make a choice between the children of her first marriage and him.

Predictably, being Hillary, she had chosen him. But then, Hillary had never been a particularly maternal woman. They had married impetuously and without really knowing one another, and Saul still felt guilty about the fact that despite knowing how ill-equipped emotionally Hillary was to cope with two small children, how resentful of them she felt, he had given in to her desire to have a third child to try to mend their failing marriage.

But much as he might regret the reasons for Meg's conception, Meg herself he could never regret, and he was determined that she would never know that in many ways she had been the final nail in the coffin of her parents' faltering marriage.

"I never wanted children. I don't like children," Hillary had stormed petulantly at him during one of their all too frequent rows.

And Saul was ashamed now to remember that he had retaliated equally bad-temperedly. "Well, you certainly don't seem to like mine."

His. Well, they were certainly his by law as well as by birth.

"But how will you cope?" Ann, his mother, had asked him anxiously when he had initially told her of his decision to fight for full custody of the children. "I'll do what I can, of course, but…"

"Look," Saul had told his mother, "you and

Dad have your own lives to lead. We all know how much Dad is looking forward to retiring. I'll manage, don't worry."

And so far he had, but there *were* times, like tonight for instance, when his regular babysitter couldn't make it and he was forced to swallow his pride and turn to his family for extra help.

One answer, of course, would be to employ someone full time to live in, but he didn't want the children to feel that he was offloading them onto someone else and he certainly didn't want them to start thinking that he didn't either love or want them and especially not little Meg, who had come back from the States so heartbreakingly insecure and clingy.

"Did you have a nice time at Auntie Livvy's?" Meg asked him.

"Very nice, thank you," Saul fibbed.

When Olivia had telephoned him to invite him over for dinner and to tell him excitedly about her friend who was relocating to work for the same firm as him, reminding him that they had previously met both at her and Caspar's wedding and Amelia's christening, he had had no intimation or warning of what the evening held in store.

Yes, he remembered Tullah. What red-blooded

heterosexual man would not? She had the kind of looks, the kind of figure, that was instantly appealing to the male psyche. There was something about that combination of thick, lustrous hair, creamy skin and wonderfully curvy body that suggested a sensuality, a lushness that had a far more instant and dizzying effect on male hormones than any bone-thin, media-lauded model-type of woman.

What man looking at Tullah's full, soft mouth and her even fuller and softer breasts could resist imagining what it would be like to lose himself in the sheer pleasure of touching her, caressing her, kissing her, making love with her?

Politically incorrect such thoughts might be, but they *were* undoubtedly an important part of what made a man a man, and to Saul's mind at least, tolerably acceptable as long as they remained restrained and controlled in the male mind. But then, as he had discovered tonight, Tullah had her own inimitable way of ensuring that any private male fantasies involving herself were very quickly squashed.

Perhaps it was the shock of the contrast between the soft, feminine lushness and apparent warmth of her body and the antagonistic, almost aggressive sharpness of her manner that had made him feel so taken aback by her obvious hostility towards him, or perhaps it was simply a rebel male gene of vanity because she was so plainly dismissive and contemptuous of him. He didn't know. What he *did* know was that he had a hard time fighting with himself not to respond to her aggressive and spiked remarks both as a defendant and a protagonist.

And the problem wasn't confined to the fact that she was simply a friend of Olivia's. There were other complications. She was going to be working for the same organisation and…

Meg made the little snuffling sound that meant that she had finally fallen asleep. As he bent down to gently kiss her cheek and tuck her in, Saul wondered wryly what on earth he had done to offend fate so much that she insisted on sending him so many problems.

First his marriage to Hillary and then the problem he was currently facing with Louise and now this. Tiredly he made his way back to his own bedroom, throwing his robe onto a chair before pushing back the covers and getting into bed.

It was ironic the effect a bad marriage—a bad *relationship*—could have on you. He now actually enjoyed sleeping alone. It was a relief to wake up in the morning without Hillary there next to him, both of them ready to begin the next round in their ongoing battle.

Wearily he closed his eyes.

Saul groaned pleasurably in his sleep, inhaling a deep, sensual breath of the delicious scent of the woman in his arms; she smelled not of some expensive designer perfume but of her own special, deeply feminine and intensely erotic scent. He had been aware of it and *her* all through dinner and had ached then to do as he was doing right now, breathing in the scent of her; he tasted it on his lips as he kissed the soft curve of her throat, nibbled his way along her jaw towards her mouth.

Her hair was a heavy, silky dark cloud of satin softness where it lay against his skin as subtly perfumed as the rest of her, her arms as rounded and smooth as the intoxicatingly female contours of her breasts. He deliberately delayed allowing himself the longed-for pleasure of kissing her mouth.

Drawing his lips along the velvet softness of her inner arm, he felt her whole body quiver as he gently caressed the inside of her elbow with the tip of his tongue until she wrenched her arm away from him to wrap both of them tightly around him and begged him to make love to her "properly."

"Properly…what do you mean properly…what is properly?" he teased her huskily whilst she pressed herself closer and even closer to him, the hard points of her breasts pushing against his skin, driving him insane with their sensual demand for attention.

"Stop talking and kiss me," she whispered, her palm insistently turning his face towards her own, her lips already parting….

"Mmm…" Saul stroked his hand down the side of her body, trying not to allow himself to linger anywhere, not even on the satin warmth of the inside of her thigh when she trembled as he caressed her. "Oh, I'm going to kiss you all right, Tullah," he told her thickly. She gave another soft, protesting moan and writhed eagerly against him. "I'm going to kiss you until that deliciously soft, irresistible mouth of yours is—"

"Daddy…daddy. Wake up. I feel sick…."

Reluctantly Saul opened his eyes and blinked dazedly up at his son.

"I feel sick," Robert repeated urgently. "I—"

"Yes, all right…come on…." Saul was already

on his feet, swinging Robert up into his arms and hurrying towards the bathroom with him.

Robert had had a very severe bout of infant gastroenteritis as a baby, so severe, in fact, that at one point their doctor had warned them that he might not survive. He had, but with the legacy of a digestive system that was acutely sensitive. They made it just in time.

Saul knew from experience that Robert's bouts of sickness were wrenching but thankfully short-lived. However, it certainly looked as though he wasn't going to get much more sleep tonight, which probably wasn't a bad thing, given the nature of the extremely erotic and extraordinarily inappropriate dream Robert had woken him from.

The subconscious was an odd thing, a very odd thing, he decided before firmly banishing the enticing, lingering image his mind had conjured up of Tullah lying voluptuously naked in his bed, still warm from their shared lovemaking.

That he should have dreamt about her at all was bad enough, but that he had been enjoying the dream so much, had been so aroused by it, so determined to hang on to it that he had fought against waking up and responding to Robert, was even worse.

He couldn't remember the last time he had had a dream like that. In fact, if he was honest with himself, he couldn't remember *any* time he had been so intensely and so physically aroused. Not even with—

"Daddy..."

"It's OK, Robert."

Sternly rebuking himself for his thoughts, he turned to minister to his son.

CHAPTER THREE

"AND I'll keep my fingers crossed that the offer you've made on the cottage is accepted," Olivia promised as she gave Tullah a goodbye hug.

As she returned it, Tullah was guiltily aware of the fact that she had not exactly been the perfect weekend guest. It went against her whole credo for living to be manipulative or underhand in any way. She couldn't pretend to share Olivia's rose-tinted view of her cousin Saul, but neither did she want to leave without at least making some attempt to explain to Olivia why she felt so antagonistic towards his type.

"Livvy, about last night," she began a little awkwardly. "I realise that you probably thought I was overreacting with Saul and—"

"Well, you did rather surprise me," Olivia admitted ruefully as she interrupted her. "You're certainly the first woman I've ever known to react to Saul in *quite* that way." Tullah opened her mouth to point out that at least one other woman must share her animosity towards him, otherwise he wouldn't be divorced, but before she could say anything, Olivia was continuing cheerfully, "Mind you, it's probably just as well. The situation's difficult enough at the moment with Louise deep in the throes of an intense crush on him."

"Yes," Tullah sympathised readily. "I appreciate that that must be an awful situation for…for her parents. I could see how distressed Jenny looked last night when Saul asked her when Louise was coming home."

All the distaste and disapproval she felt about Saul's behaviour in not just allowing but actively encouraging Louise's crush on him showed in Tullah's voice as she spoke.

"It's typical of the kind of man that the Sauls of this world are that he didn't even think twice about how he might be offending or hurting Jon and Jenny by introducing the subject of Louise. It was obvious that they weren't at all happy with the situation and who could blame them?

"I mean, I *know* he's your cousin, Livvy," Tullah told her fiercely, her emotions darkening her eyes as she remembered how she had felt for the older couple the previous evening. "But what kind of man…what kind of decent, caring, mature man who feels good about himself as a man and who feels really at ease with his masculinity, his sexuality, experiences the need to keep on massaging his ego by seducing a string of younger and younger naïve girls?"

As Tullah paused for breath, she saw that Olivia was looking rather shocked.

"I'm sorry," she apologised contritely. "I know, of course, that you probably don't share my views and that your opinion of Saul is bound to be different from mine especially in view of the…the relationship you and he—"

"Tullah, Saul and I—" Olivia began, only to break off in maternal concern as Amelia, who had been playing quite happily a few yards away in the garden, let out a frightened cry. "Oh no! She's probably trying to catch another bee," she told Tullah. "Amelia darling…"

"Oh dear," Tullah sympathised as they exchanged another brief hug and stepped back from each other, leaving Olivia free to go and rescue both the indignant bee and her small daughter whilst Tullah got into her car.

"I think I've discovered why Tullah is so antagonistic towards Saul," Olivia commented to

Caspar over dinner several hours after Tullah had left.

"Mmm… You mean there *is* a reason and it isn't just that she's a woman of incomparable taste and good sense who couldn't help but prefer me?" Caspar joked.

"No, I'm afraid I cornered the market in that particular brand of good taste and sense," Olivia informed him gravely, trying not to giggle.

"Oh well, go on, then. What deeply traumatic reason lies behind her aversion?"

"It isn't funny, Caspar," Olivia warned him. "At least it isn't when you know about Tullah's background. Her parents divorced when she was in her teens, and very shortly after that an older man…a family friend, in fact, on whom she'd got a massive crush, instead of realising that what she was really looking for was a father substitute, someone to treat her gently and give her the nonsexual love her father had deprived her of, decided instead to use Tullah's innocence and naïvety to boost his own flagging ego.

"She was only sixteen at the time and she believed he loved her. He told her that his marriage was over, the usual kind of thing, and of course, she fell for it and she now seems to have jumped to the totally wrong conclusion that Saul is doing exactly the same thing to Louise as this man did to her."

"Ahh...I'm beginning to see daylight. You put her right, of course," Caspar commented as he helped himself to a second helping of pudding.

"No...Amelia tried her latest bee-catching trick before I could and then by the time I'd rescued the bee and calmed Amelia down, it was too late. Tullah had left. Do you really think you should eat that?" she asked her husband conversationally. "All that cream will be loaded with cholesterol, and you—"

"I need the energy," Caspar told her. "Or have you changed your mind about enlivening our incipient bee-keeper's life with a little bit of sibling rivalry?"

"Not at all," Olivia responded, adding provocatively, "but if we're going to do that, I can think of far better uses to put that cream to...."

"Such as?" Caspar invited.

"I thought you weren't going to make it," Olivia commented warmly to Saul as he and the children joined them in the departures lounge.

The whole family had gathered to wave Ruth

and Grant off for their regular biannual visit to the States.

After fifty years apart with each believing the other had betrayed their love, they were now happily reunited, and in keeping with the spirit of the mock prenuptial agreement both of them constantly teased the other with, they had fallen into a pleasant routine of spending three months in Haslewich followed by three months in Grant's home town in New England.

It was Bobbie, Ruth's American granddaughter and her cousin Luke's wife, who would miss them the most, Olivia acknowledged. For this trip a very special concession was being made for Joss, Jon and Jenny's younger son who had always been especially close to Ruth, who together with Jack, Olivia's own brother, was being allowed to go with the older couple and spend some time with the New England side of the family.

"Mmm…I was afraid we wouldn't make it," Saul responded after he had hugged Ruth warmly and shaken Grant by the hand. "Robert had another bad night."

"Oh dear, is he…?"

"He's fine now," Saul assured her, anticipating her question and nodding in the direction of his three children who were huddled in a small group with all the younger members of the family, including Joss and Jack.

"What with Robert's sickness and Meg's nightmares, you can't be getting much sleep," Olivia sympathised.

"Nowhere near enough," Saul agreed ruefully, "and not just because of the kids."

But when Olivia looked questioningly at him he simply shook his head. There was no way he was going to enlighten even someone as close to him as Olivia about the fact that his sleep had been broken not just by the children but far more disturbingly by dreams about her weekend guest, dreams of such intense sensuality and sexuality that if he hadn't been a mature man in his thirties he would have blushed to even have recalled them.

"Oh, Gramps…I so wish I was going with you," Bobbie wailed, hugging her grandfather tightly as the notice flashed up to say that their plane was boarding.

"Thanks a lot," Luke, her husband, teased her ruefully, looking round for someone to hand their baby daughter to whilst he comforted his wife.

"Here, let me take her," Saul offered, deftly

taking the child from him and expertly settling her comfortably against his shoulder as his own Meg sidled up to him and slipped her small hand into his.

"Can I have a look at Francesca?" she asked him. As she studied the sleeping baby, Meg informed him chattily, "My friend Grace at school, well, her mummy's going to have a baby. Will we ever have a new baby, Daddy?" she asked him, crinkling her forehead.

"Don't be stupid, Meg. Only mummies can have babies and we..."

Saul grimaced to himself as Robert overheard their conversation and spoke scornfully to his younger sister.

"I'm not stupid," Meg responded heatedly, "am I, Daddy?"

Jemima, his elder daughter, eyed them both with disfavour. His little Jem, Saul called her, and in many ways he felt that the break-up of their marriage had been the hardest for her to cope with. At eight, she was mature mentally for her years and just beginning to grasp the concept of the intricacies of adult relationships and to know that adults were not infallible.

He had always felt that she was more her

mother's child than his, and it had surprised him to discover how passionately and intensely she had wanted to return to England and to him.

"Our mother won't have any more babies," she informed her siblings sharply. "She doesn't like children."

Saul caught his breath.

What Jemima had said in essence was the truth. Hillary did *not* like children and she had already informed him that since her new husband did not like them, either, she had decided to be sterilised.

"Something I should have done before I married you," she had told him starkly and more than a little bitterly when she had informed him that she wasn't going to contest his having full custody of the children.

"She loves you," he told the three of them now as they watched him. And how could it not be true? Hillary might not *like* children but surely she must love her own. What mother could not do?

At eight, seven and five, their three had, he accepted, been conceived too closely together for a woman who was not particularly maternal. He accepted, too, that the larger part of the responsibility for them in their early years, especially Jemima and Robert, had fallen on Hillary.

With Meg it had been different; their last-ditch attempt to rescue their marriage and cement it together with Meg's conception had been a sanity-threatening mistake and grossly unfair to Meg herself.

Six weeks after her birth, he had arrived home one afternoon, prompted by heaven alone knew what paternal sixth sense, to find Hillary on the point of leaving for America—without the children and without apparently having any intention of telling him what she was doing.

Later that day, having failed to persuade Hillary to change her mind, he had gone to pick the children up from the child-minder and had promised them mentally then that even if he might have failed as a husband and a lover, he would not fail them as a father…a parent….

"When is Louise coming to see us again?" Meg asked later when they were on their way home. "I like her."

"She doesn't like you," Jemima sniffed disparagingly. "She only comes round to see Dad, really."

"Jem..." Saul warned her, glancing in the rear-view mirror to give her a stern look whilst he monitored Meg's quivering bottom lip.

They were just so vulnerable...all of them in their different ways. Meg with her fear of the dark, clinging to him, Rob who thought that boys shouldn't cry and who made himself sick instead, and Jem...big, brave, cynical Jemima who wrung his heart with her studied and oh so heartachingly fragile defence of contemptuous disdain mixed with anger.

Listening to Tullah on Saturday night had reminded him of Jemima.

Tullah...

Don't start that, he warned himself. You've got enough problems without going looking for any more.

"It's amazing to think Louise and Katie's first year at college will be over soon," Jenny reflected to Jon as they drove home from seeing Ruth and Grant off.

"I know," Jon replied.

"I was hoping that now Louise is at university she'd start to grow out of this crush she's got on Saul. He's been so good about it. She worries me sometimes, Jon. She's so headstrong and so single-minded."

"Tell me about it," Jon returned dryly. "She's a Crighton all right, through and through."

"I'm afraid she's going to have a hard life ahead of her if she doesn't learn to bend a little," Jenny sighed. "It's hard to believe that she and Katie are twins. At times they're so different temperamentally."

"Not so hard, surely," Jon commented. "Look at David and me."

Jenny glanced at her husband. After all these years and all that David had done, Jon still put his twin ahead of himself even when he spoke about him.

"Do you think we'll ever hear from him again?" she asked, referring to the fact that while recovering from a severe heart attack Jon's brother and Olivia's father had simply walked out of their lives without any explanation. That was over three years ago now and they still hadn't heard anything definite from him.

"Who knows? For Dad's sake, I wish and hope we do. He won't admit it, you know how stubborn the old man is, but I think he suspects that it wasn't just the pressure of Tiggy's illness that made David leave. We can't risk telling him the whole truth, of course, but he's changed since David left. He's still as stubborn as he always was, but now it's as though he's clinging to that stubbornness like a crutch he needs to support himself with instead of using it like a stick to beat the rest of us."

Jenny laughed.

"Ben *is* getting older," she reminded her husband.

"Aren't we all," Jon retorted feelingly.

"What are we going to do about Louise?" Jenny prodded him. "The last time she was home she made a positive nuisance of herself with Saul, inviting herself to go and stay with Hugh and Ann like that and then… And now with Saul living so close, it's going to be even worse."

"She's *your* daughter," Jon told her tongue-in-cheek, adding mock-virtuously, "and it's a mother's duty."

"She's *your* daughter, as well," Jenny lost no time in retaliating, concluding triumphantly, "and as you've just said yourself, she is quite definitely a Crighton. All joking aside, Jon, we're going to have to do something…say something. If it was Katie, for instance, she'd be mortified at the thought of anyone knowing how she felt, but on the other hand she would never pursue anyone the way Louise is pursuing Saul."

Jon nodded his agreement. "It's a pity Ruth's going to be away while she's home. She's very good at that sort of thing. Of course, the best thing would be for Saul to find himself someone else…get married again."

"Saul marry again?" Jenny frowned. "Do you think he would? It hit him very hard when he and Hillary broke up. I remember him telling me at the time that he felt as though he had failed. Not just failed Hillary and himself and the children, but his parents, the family, his upbringing and his beliefs…everything. He as good as said that even knowing he didn't love Hillary any more he'd have been prepared to continue with the marriage for the sake of the children.

"What did you think of Olivia's weekend guest, by the way," Jenny asked her husband in amusement. "She was very anti Saul, wasn't she?"

"Was she?" Jon asked, a fatuous semi-glazed expression enveloping his face. "I didn't pay much attention to what she *said*," he admitted, grinning at Jenny.

"It's just as well you're the one driving this car,"

Jenny warned him, "otherwise I'd be tempted to push you out. *Why* is it that when a man sees a more than averagely pretty girl he immediately forgets that she's also a fully functioning, intelligent and equal human being?"

"I didn't forget," Jon protested in a mock-injured tone. "Obviously she's intelligent…and very highly qualified, but you've got to admit that she's…well, she's…"

"Sexy," Jenny suggested with dangerous sweetness.

"Sexy." Jon rolled his eyes. "That's like describing the Grand Canyon as a valley. She's—"

"Stop drooling, Jon," Jenny advised. "It makes you look senile. Mind you," she added fair-mindedly, "I have to say that she came across very much to me as a woman's woman. Hardly the type to flirt or make use of her, er, assets."

"No, she was a bit on the serious side. Still, living in Haslewich will probably help her to ease down a gear or two. By the way, when are Max and Madeleine next due to visit?" he asked.

Jenny gave him a shrewd look.

Max, their elder son, was a fast-track barrister with a prestigious set of London chambers. He was also the epitome of his uncle David with most of his faults and several more of his own thrown in. Add to that the fact that he was a handsome and highly sexed young man married to a very sweet but rather plain young woman whose sole claim on his affections was the fact that she was the daughter of a prominent High Court judge with a Law Lord for a grandfather.

Include in the recipe the highly volatile ingredients of a young baby, whom Max made no secret of not having wanted, and several rich and well-connected female clients whom, if the gossip they had heard was correct, he had been equally open about not only wanting but actually *having* and it was no wonder that Jenny should feel her heart start to sink at the thought of Max coming into contact with Tullah.

He would lay seige to her, of course, because quite simply he was that kind of man, but thankfully Tullah had not struck her as the kind of woman who would come anywhere near being tempted to respond.

As he heard her sigh, Jon looked at his wife with a twinkle in his eyes. "Well, it certainly isn't from me that *your* son and *your* daughter get their high-octane sex drives," he told her virtuously.

Jenny's mouth had started to form a round O of

rebuttal before she realised he was teasing her, but once she did she simply smiled at him and said softly, "Oh no? What about last night, then?"

"What about it?" Jon asked innocently, but he was blushing slightly and Jenny shook her head as she reminded him, "*I* wasn't the one who had to lie to Joss and Jack that I needed an extra hour in bed because I'd got a headache."

"No. But you still came up with me," he reminded her.

"That was my duty as your wife," she retaliated firmly. "After all, a man of your age…a headache could be…could be…"

"An excuse to get my wife into bed so that I could make love to her," Jon suggested softly, adding, "Well, *tonight* we won't *need* an excuse, will we? We've got the house to ourselves."

"*Twice* in one week," Jenny mock protested.

"What do you mean, twice in one week," Jon growled back. "We went past that last night!"

"Well, that's the last of them." Sitting back on her heels, Tullah smiled as she looked across the neatly stacked boxes at her mother. "Thanks for coming to help me." She shook her head as she added ruefully, "I had no idea I owned so much stuff."

"Well, you can't get to nearly thirty without accumulating some possessions," her mother responded.

Tullah gave her a wry look. "You're just sorry that I don't happen to number a husband and a couple of children amongst mine, is that it?" she teased.

Despite the break-up of her first marriage after Tullah's father had left her for his secretary, Jean had remained incurably romantic, marrying a second time when Tullah was in her early twenties after a whirlwind courtship with a man she had met whilst on holiday.

Tullah liked her stepfather, who adored and doted on her mother. He was a kind, gentle man whose first wife had died ten years before he and her mother had met, and was nothing like her father.

"It isn't that I wish you were married, darling," Jean told her now. "It's just...well, I can't help feeling if your father and I hadn't divorced and if that dreadful man hadn't—"

"The divorce wasn't your fault," Tullah reminded her, "and, as for that dreadful man... I should have realised what he really was instead of being so gullible."

"Darling, you were sixteen," her mother protested. "Still, perhaps now you're moving out of London you might meet someone nice."

"I doubt it. Haslewich is Crighton territory and judging by the—"

"Crighton territory?" Jean looked puzzled.

Tullah laughed. "Sorry," she apologised. "Just my little joke. Olivia Crighton as she was then, whom I used to work with, lives in Haslewich. Her family come from the area."

"Olivia…oh yes, you went to her wedding."

"And her daughter's christening. She invited me to stay with her last month when I went to Haslewich to meet the relocation agent."

After getting to her feet, Tullah went into the small kitchen of her soon-to-be ex-flat and started to fill the kettle.

"Oh? You don't sound as though you enjoyed it. Didn't the two of you get on?"

"Oh, we got on. It's just that Olivia has this cousin…of a sort. There are so many of them, I'm not quite sure how Saul slots into place."

Her mother came to join her in the kitchen.

"Decaff for me, darling, if that's coffee you're making," she instructed. "But *who* is Saul?"

Tullah hid a small smile. Her mother was, if not subtle, certainly disarmingly difficult to sidetrack.

"Saul is...Saul," she told her uninformatively, pouring the boiling water into the coffee mugs. As she handed one to her mother, she added quietly, "He's another Ralph...only worse."

Tullah paused and frowned before taking a sip of her coffee, then explained the situation.

"He's got children of his own, three of them, two girls and a boy," Tullah eventually finished by saying. "So you'd think as a parent he'd understand at least some of what Jenny and Jon must be feeling."

"What's he like? Is he good-looking?"

Tullah studied her mother warily. Sometimes, even now, Jean's astuteness still had the power to surprise her. Maternal instinct or simply a personality trait? Tullah wasn't sure. She only knew that she had never been more glad of anything than when her mother had told her gently that she had guessed what was going on with Ralph and had invited Tullah to tell her all about it.

The pain of discovering that she had been

cheated—that she was not loved by Ralph—might have faded long ago along with her own adolescent feelings for him, but the humiliation, the anguish, the guilt she had suffered, were still there even if time had tempered them somewhat. To know that her mother understood, that she wasn't rejecting her, that she believed in her, had been the only saving grace of the whole sorry episode.

"Mmm...I suppose so," she confirmed noncommittally now, but she still couldn't quite meet her mother's eyes and had to turn away to pretend to study the kitchen tiles to avoid looking directly at her as she added, "If you like the type, and personally I don't. Anyway," she concluded defensively, "I think it's very shallow to be attracted to a man simply because of the way he looks."

"Oh, very," her mother agreed seriously and then spoiled it all by starting to giggle.

"Mother," Tullah reproved, but she couldn't help smiling herself.

"Well, you *are* right," Jean conceded when they had both stopped laughing. "A handsome face and even a good body aren't worth much unless they are backed up by—"

"A good brain," Tullah interposed sternly.

"Well...a kind heart at least," her mother concurred. "But...is he sexy?" she asked mischievously.

"Sexy..." Tullah tried to look reproving but failed, her eyes gleaming with the same amusement that lightened her mother's.

All three of them, her sister included, shared the rare gift of a similar sense of fun and lightheartedness, linking them in a way that had excluded their far less good-humoured father.

"Well, he *has* got three children," she told her mother mock-innocently.

"That doesn't prove anything. Anyone can—"

"Yes, all right. He's sexy," Tullah affirmed and then fell silent, astonished not just by her admission but even more by her previously suppressed and intensely feminine recognition of something that, to anyone else, she would have sworn she had never even noticed.

"So...he's good-looking, he's sexy...and he's got three children. Tell me again what's wrong with him," her mother said, having ticked these assets off on her fingers.

"He's divorced...he's...he's another Ralph and I just don't like him," Tullah supplied for her.

"Mmm...well, does Olivia have any *other* male cousins?"

"Mother!" Tullah warned.

"All right," Jean accepted placidly. "But you can't blame me for trying. I'm not getting any younger. I want to enjoy my grandchildren and—All right, all right...now which of these boxes do you want us to store for you and which are you taking with you?"

"I'm going to have to leave most of this stuff with you for the time being," Tullah told her. "Until the cottage has been rewired and replumbed, I'm virtually going to be living in one room."

Once she had got over the shock of having her offer for the cottage accepted, what had stunned her even more was the thrill of excitement and anticipation she had felt at knowing that it was going to be hers. An urban career girl up until now, her flat had simply been somewhere to sleep and eat. The thought of ever wanting some place she could call a "home' had been a totally alien concept, but now she was guiltily conscious of the glossy magazines tucked carefully away out of sight and the brochures featuring gleaming, richly enamelled traditional farmhouse ovens that she had taken to pouring avidly over ever since she had fallen in love with Olivia's warm burgundy Aga.

She had also fallen equally deeply in love with Olivia's two-year-old daughter, she reminded herself waspishly, but that hadn't sent her dashing out to stare covetously through the windows of baby equipment shops or to…

Her mother smiled. "Lucinda is convinced that Stafford is starting to smile properly."

Tullah stared at her mother. *How* did she do it? She was sometimes convinced that her mother was a close relation to a white witch. Just *how* did she manage to so unerringly pick up on her own train of thought? Carefully she scrutinised her mother's face. No sign of any guile there, but why choose *that* particular moment to mention her sister's new baby.

"He isn't old enough to smile properly yet," she retorted promptly and then cursed herself under her breath as she caught her mother's jaw dropping. "Livvy happened to mention that babies didn't smile properly until they were at least six weeks old," she told her defensively, "and Stafford is only ten days old."

"You smiled from the day you were born," her mother told her serenely.

Tullah gave her a withering look.

"Saul..." her mother mused. "It's such a strong, purposeful name for a man, isn't it? Sort of dependable...reliable..."

"Good father material, you mean," Tullah returned with acid sweetness. "I'll bet his three children think so," she added hotly, "when they're being packed off back to their mother just as soon as he can get rid of them. It beats me *why* men like him are always so determined to hang on to their custody rights. Well, it doesn't, of course. Most of the time they do it just to upset their ex-wives."

"Tullah," her mother protested, "you don't know."

"I know that he couldn't even give up a few hours away from a family dinner party to be with them," Tullah told her fiercely, "and that's enough for me."

"It's just as well you decided to go into industry," her mother opined. "If you'd ever made it on to the Bench you'd quite definitely have been called the hanging judge."

"Yes, and guess what I'd like to see men like the Saul Crightons of this world hang by," Tullah retorted sweetly.

CHAPTER FOUR

"AND now I'll take you upstairs to introduce you to our new boss."

"New boss?" Tullah queried as she started to follow the colleague who had been showing her round her new work area.

"Yes, there's been a bit of a reshuffle. Neil Radcliffe, who used to head the department, has been transferred to New York and his place has been taken by the ex-deputy head of our international section, Saul Crighton. You'll like him. It's a bit of a sideways move for Saul, but he's a single father with three young children to look after. Our European operation isn't quite so far from home as the States if he was needed in an emergency."

"Saul Crighton..." Tullah couldn't help repeating as she ignored the latter part of Barbara's speech.

"Yes," the other woman responded, pausing

as she pressed the button for the lift. "Is there something wrong?"

"No," Tullah assured her untruthfully.

Saul Crighton was her new boss. Had he known that night Olivia had invited him to dinner, and if he had known, why hadn't he said something to her?

Why...because he was *that* kind of man, that's why, Tullah fumed as the lift bell pinged and the door opened to admit them. Because *being* that kind of man he would have enjoyed listening to her digging her own professional grave.

Well, department head or not, it was the *company* who was employing her and not him personally. The company who was employing them *both*. But her self-reassurances had a decidedly hollow ring, Tullah admitted as she recalled the grim look she had seen on Saul's face as he overheard her criticisms of him.

Well, it was too late to do anything about that now, but despite her straight back and determinedly lifted chin, her legs felt decidedly weak and unsteady as she followed her new colleague out of the lift and down the corridor with the door at the end of it marked "Saul Crighton, Director'.

Director. Tullah swallowed. Olivia hadn't said anything to her about Saul's being elected to the Board.

Barbara knocked briefly on the door and then opened it. She led Tullah into a surprisingly comfortable rather than an opulently furnished office occupied by a smiling middle-aged woman who greeted them both warmly and introduced herself as Saul's secretary, Marsha.

"He isn't here at the moment," she informed Tullah, "but if you'd like to wait he shouldn't be too long."

He wasn't. Tullah had barely read more than a couple of paragraphs of an article on the front page of that day's *Financial Times* when the outer door opened and Saul came in dressed not, as she had expected, in a formal business suit but in a pair of snug-fitting, *extremely* snug-fitting jeans, she noticed as he walked past her, and a soft white cotton shirt with the sleeves rolled back and open at the throat, his hair slightly tousled as though he had just run rather walked in a leisurely top-executive manner from his car to the building.

"Tullah," he greeted her with a smile, extending his hand towards her as she stood up and reluctantly faced him. "I'm sorry you've had to wait. A small crisis at home."

"One of the children?" his secretary sympathised understandingly.

Saul gave her a rueful look. "In one sense yes. The latest addition to the household somehow or other arranged to get hold of a disk I hadn't filed."

"Oh dear…"

"Oh dear indeed," Saul agreed dryly, explaining for Tullah's benefit, "I rather misguidedly promised the children a dog. I'd forgotten what sharp teeth young puppies have and how much looking after they need. This one is still missing his mother and he's very determined to let us all know about it. He cries all night, every night."

"You'll have to wrap a ticking clock in his blanket," Tullah informed him without thinking. He looked quizzically at her and asked, "Why, what purpose does that serve? Intelligent though animals are, I doubt that a ticking clock is going to remind this particular specimen that he ought to be asleep."

"Maybe not," Tullah concurred coolly, "but it *will* remind him of the comfort of feeling and hearing his mother's heartbeat."

"Ah…yes…of course." Saul's mouth curled up slightly at the edges.

She had been wrong when she told her mother he was good-looking, Tullah acknowledged. This man was more than merely good-looking, he was…

He was another Ralph, she reminded herself sternly, a divorcé who apparently had thought nothing of breaking his marriage vows by getting involved with Olivia and, even worse, encouraging Louise.

"That is an excellent idea. I'll have to try tonight, otherwise—"

"It can't be easy," Marsha interrupted him with a smile. "He'll be keeping the children awake as well as you."

"Well, yes…he would have been…" Saul paused and gave her a shamefaced look. "I gave in last night and let him come upstairs with me. I think you could be right about the alarm clock," he told Tullah. "I woke up this morning to find that he'd managed to scramble on to the bed and made himself very comfortable, thank you, tucked up on top of the bed next to me. That will certainly have to stop. I've only just been able to persuade

Meg that the proper place to sleep is in her own bedroom."

The sympathy Tullah had weak-mindedly been feeling for him evaporated as she decided grimly that the reason he didn't want his daughter in his room was probably because he had someone rather older and with a very different purpose in mind to share it with.

What was *wrong* with her, she chided herself mentally, going all soft and gooey just because of the sentimental images he had conjured up in her mind—memories of her own dog at home and the way she would illicitly let her into her room despite being forbidden to do so.

"I've just about got time to shower and change before my meeting with Paul and then I'll go over those notes this afternoon before I fly out to Brussels."

"I'll make you some coffee," his secretary announced, bustling out from behind her desk.

"Please," Saul agreed, giving Marsha a smile that made Tullah's mouth curl contemptuously and her toes curl in a very different reaction altogether. *Why* was it that her body so ridiculously and stubbornly refused to acknowledge what her brain was trying to tell it? she wondered crossly as she felt her body's reaction to Saul's proximity jolt right through her.

She could even smell him, she decided distastefully, but it wasn't really distaste at all that motivated her to take a step back from him, and the scent she could smell clinging to his skin wasn't unpleasant, far from it. In fact… She swallowed hard, turning her head away just to make sure she was out of range of that irritating, subtle, havoc-wreaking blend of maleness that was having such an unwanted effect on her senses.

"We've got a very good team here on our European side of things, Tullah," Saul told her, "and I very much hope that you'll enjoy being a part of it."

A welcome or warning? Tullah wondered once he had nodded his head briefly in dismissal of her and stridden by her into his own private office. He had left the door open, though, and as she walked past it she couldn't resist the impulse to glance towards it—and then wished she hadn't.

En route to what was obviously his private bathroom, he had discarded his shirt, pausing only to open a concealed wardrobe in the office's panelling to reveal the white shirts and formal suits she had expected to see him wearing.

The muscles in his back flexed as he reached up to remove fresh clothes. His skin had a warm, even tan and she caught herself wondering just how far below the waistband of his trousers it actually went, then stopped, aghast by the direction her thoughts were taking and equally shocked by the way she was standing gawping. But that was nothing to what she felt as Saul unexpectedly turned round and looked at her as though he had been aware that she was still standing there. His expression was unreadable whilst she knew shamingly that hers was all *too* readable as she started to colour up hotly and had to turn and walk quickly towards the door in an effort to escape both his scrutiny of her and her own embarrassment.

"Oh no."

"Something wrong?" Tullah asked Barbara sympathetically as the young woman suddenly let out an agonised wail of dismay.

"You could say that," she confirmed ruefully. "I've got a dentist's appointment in half an hour, which I'll just about make if I leave now, and I've just realised that the report Saul asked me to let him have by four is still here on my desk.

I thought I'd taken it up with the other stuff he wanted." She gave Tullah a pleading look. "You wouldn't take it up for me, would you? It's just if I don't leave now I know I'm going to be late and my dentist has a bit of a thing about punctuality. I've already missed my last two appointments. I daren't miss another."

How could she refuse? Tullah acknowledged to herself.

"You're an angel and I promise I'll return the favour with interest," Barbara told her fervently, pulling on her jacket and reaching for her bag as she did so.

Once she had gone, Tullah eyed the report she had left behind with disfavour. So far she had not had to have too much contact with Saul and that was the way she wanted to keep it.

She picked up the report and headed for the corridor. With any luck he might not be in his office anyway. And if he was… If he was, all she had to do was hand him the report and leave.

As she walked towards Saul's office, the air-conditioning in the corridor made her shiver slightly and regret that she had not taken the time to slip her suit jacket on over her thin silk blouse.

His secretary's office door was open, but there

was no sign of her at her desk and no sign, either, of Saul in the room that lay beyond it, Tullah noted in relief as she glanced warily through the open door.

Quickly she stepped inside the room and headed straight for Saul's desk, fully intending to simply place the file on it and leave again, but as she did so, a press cutting covering an interesting case she had been following through the European courts caught her eye and she automatically paused to read it. If won, the case would set an important new precedent in the field of international law and Tullah was so engrossed in what she was reading that even when, out of the corner of her eye, she saw the door opposite her opening, she didn't really register what was happening until she saw Saul emerge and realised from his still dampened, very nearly totally naked state, apart from the towel he had wrapped around his hips, that he had come out of his private bathroom.

His sharp "Tullah, what are you doing here?" followed by the frowning look he gave her, did nothing to help the colour burning her face to subside.

Hastily she tried to look away, to look anywhere but at him—at a body that she now was very well aware was far too boldly masculine to be openly paraded in front of her in the way that he was doing. He must be preparing to go out for the evening. It was most unfortunate that she had caught him, a second time, in a state of undress. And it galled her even more to realise that of the two of them *she* was the one who felt uncomfortable and embarrassed whilst he…

"I…I was just leaving," she announced hurriedly, starting to move away from the desk.

"No, you weren't," Saul returned promptly.

Tullah tensed as he walked towards her, looking past her to his desk, obviously wanting to see what had captured her attention.

"Ah, the Epsberg case," he declared. "Have you been following it?"

"Er, yes…I have," Tullah affirmed.

Why in heaven's name didn't he go and put some clothes on? Didn't he *know, realise…*? She swallowed hard, transfixed to the spot by what she later firmly assured herself had been total astonishment and not some kind of weak-kneed and very dangerous female response to the sight of that dark-haired, damp and very strong forearm reaching past her to pick up the piece she had just been reading.

"Mmm…so what's your opinion of how the final verdict is likely to go?"

"Er, I…"

No wonder he was frowning at her like that. She was behaving like a complete idiot, Tullah recognised furiously. Had the man *no* sense of… of…? How on earth did he keep his body so superbly muscled and fit? He wasn't some young athlete in his early twenties after all.

To her consternation, she suddenly heard him saying softly as though he had read her mind, "Football, with the children."

"Football?"

Somehow or other, despite her glowing face, Tullah managed to make herself look him straight in the eye.

"Really," she began, fully intending to give him the kind of verbal put-down she knew she needed to hear, even if he didn't. She had to find some way of reasserting herself and disabusing him of any idea he might have that she as a woman might be in any way aware of or aroused by his… by him…because, of course, she wasn't. Not at all…not in the least.

But before she could finish what she had been about to say, Saul continued affably, extending his arm towards her as he pointed to the fading bruise she had not even noticed. "I'm afraid so. I wasn't concentrating properly and Meg missed the ball and kicked me instead."

Tullah closed her eyes.

He thought she had been looking at his *bruise*! Thank God he had inadvertently given her that piece of information *before* she had said what she had been planning to say. She gave a small fervent shiver of relief.

"The air-conditioning in here *is* a bit keen, isn't it?" Saul commented.

"Perhaps *you* might find the temperature a little bit more hospitable if you put some clothes on," Tullah snapped back at him.

"Perhaps," Saul agreed gravely. "But it wasn't myself I was referring to. *You* shivered," he added when Tullah frowned uncomprehendingly.

"I'm not cold," Tullah denied curtly.

"No?"

The thoughtful and very thorough look Saul was giving her body made her tense warily and automatically follow his glance downwards and then stop in furious chagrin as she realised the reason for his comment.

Beneath her fine silk shirt and despite the fact

that she was wearing a bra, the protruding outline of her nipples was quite clearly visible.

The temptation to cross her arms protectively over her chest to conceal it from him was one she only just managed to resist. To let him have the last word and admit defeat galled her intensely but what else could she do?

Tell him again that she wasn't cold, that the truth was… The truth was what?

That for some unimaginable reason her body, *her* body, had taken the decision to sexually respond to him as a man without giving her the opportunity to object cerebrally or emotionally to its decision to do so.

And why? She didn't even like the man, never mind… Hastily Tullah fixed her gaze on the safe and Saul-empty space by the door to his secretary's office and started determinedly to walk towards it. Her mouth had gone dry and her heart was beating in an idiotic and ridiculously Victorian, fluttery feminine fashion.

What on earth was the matter with her? she asked herself scornfully once she had gained the relative security of the secretary's office, firmly closing the connecting door behind her as she did so. The days were gone when the sight of a man's shower-damp, naked torso had the effect of making a woman weak at the knees.

Weren't they?

CHAPTER FIVE

"YOU can forget the gym. This is far more taxing," Tullah huffed as she stroked the last brush of paint on to her newly decorated bedroom ceiling. She looked down enquiringly to where Olivia was standing watching her and asked, "What do you think? I've given it two coats now. Will it need a third?"

"No, it looks fine. Very good," Olivia assured her, putting her head to one side as she studied the freshly painted bedroom. "I really do like this sandy colour," she remarked to Tullah. "It's very soft and warm and yet not at all intrusive."

"It's from the National Trust approved range of traditional coloured paints," Tullah informed her. "I was a bit worried that it might be too pale at first, but I must admit I like it."

She climbed down the ladder and stood beside her friend to study her handiwork.

"So how's it going, apart from your aching back muscles?" Olivia teased as they made their way downstairs and into the kitchen, which was still in the process of being rewired.

"Well, as you can see, it's quite definitely got potential," Tullah told her drolly and then spoiled the effect of her mock-serious reply by starting to smile.

As they both looked around the kitchen from which the original drab sixties-style kitchen units had been removed and studied the tangle of wires and pipes protruding from the holes in the plaster, Olivia burst out laughing.

Ten minutes later when their shared laughter had subsided and they were both nursing freshly made mugs of coffee, the electrician and his mate who had just returned from their lunch break stared at them suspiciously as they both greeted his comment that the kitchen might not look much at the moment but that it definitely had potential with another fit of giggles.

"Come on," Tullah invited Olivia. "Let's go back upstairs to my bedroom. It's about the only place that's habitable at the moment." As they stood together admiring the view from Tullah's bedroom window, she mused, "Every time I wonder if my decision to buy this place was brought on by a brainstorm, I come in here and look out of this window."

"Mmm...I really do envy you this view. How are you getting on with your next-door neighbours, by the way?"

"Very well. They're marvellously kind and helpful, keeping an eye on the builders for me while I'm at work and practically insisting that I have dinner with them in the evening. They're off abroad again at the end of the month and I'm going to miss them."

"So life's treating you well and you're very pleased with your decision to move here?"

"Ninety per cent," Tullah agreed, adding mildly, "You might have warned me that Saul was going to be my new boss."

"I didn't know, not then," Olivia defended herself. "He only told us about it the week after you'd gone. It's a bit of a sideways move for him, really, but I understand why he's made it. Now that he's got custody of the children, it's only natural that he's going to want to be here for them."

"He's got *custody* of the children?" Tullah frowned. When Saul's children had been mentioned on the morning of her introduction to the company, she assumed that they must be staying with him on an extended visit. "That's rather unusual isn't it?" she queried sharply. "His wife must—"

"Hillary, his ex-wife, was the one who suggested that he have full custody," Olivia intervened quietly. "Apparently her new partner wasn't prepared to take on three children who weren't his and he as good as told Hillary that she had to choose them or him."

"And she chose *him*?"

Olivia gave a small shrug. "She was never the maternal type and made no secret of the fact that she resented having three small children on her hands."

"Poor little things. How awful for them, knowing that neither their mother nor their father really wanted them," Tullah couldn't help sympathising compassionately.

"Saul *does* want them," Olivia corrected her firmly, immediately. "But he also doesn't want there to be any acrimony between himself and Hillary for the children's sake.

"He's always held the view that their happiness and emotional well-being are more important than him and Hillary scoring points off one another by fighting over custody. But I've never seen anyone react as fast as he did when he got that phone call from Hillary telling him to come and get them one time the children were staying with her because she couldn't cope with the problems they were causing her any longer.

"I must admit, though, I was a bit surprised when he insisted that Hillary should retain virtually open visiting rights, but I suppose it does make sense if you take the long-term view, which typically Saul does.

"He believes there will come a time when the children will want to know their mother and when, in fact, she may feel she wants to get closer to them. He also says that if they continue to visit her it will take away the mystique of her being a fairy-tale parent, but at the moment all three of them are emphatic that they want to be with him. They're bound to be a bit insecure, of course, and although he doesn't make an issue of it, it can't be easy for him. Little Meg has the most appalling nightmares, Robbie has a nervous stomach, and as for Jemima, well, she's always been a slightly remote, watchful child, but I know Saul was very concerned about how withdrawn she was becoming. That was one of the major reasons why he moved here. He's a wonderful father," she told Tullah simply.

Tullah gave her a polite smile. Sing Saul's praises though she might, Olivia was not going to persuade her to change her mind about him. After all, how good a father was a man, really, when he tried openly to inveigle Olivia into an affair with him whilst he was still married.

"Look, the real reason I came over was to ask you if you'd like to have dinner with us on Saturday," Olivia announced.

Tullah gave her a suspicious look. "Saul the saviour isn't going to be there, is he?" she enquired waspishly.

"Nope, he'll be in Brussels on business," Olivia assured her, ignoring the sarcasm in her voice. "His children will be, though. They're staying over with us while he's away. It's only for a couple of nights."

"They're staying with you. Why doesn't he hire someone to live in? He can afford it, surely."

"He can afford it, yes, but what he wants for them is to grow up in a proper extended family environment. That's why he moved here in the first place. He talked the whole thing over with all of us before he committed himself to the move and we all agreed with his decision. We're *family*, Tullah," she declared firmly, "and as such we believe in helping one another out and being there for one another. That's what families do. Oh, we may quarrel and fight but at the end of the day…" She gave a small shake of her head.

"Of course Saul could afford to pay for live-in help and even if he couldn't, if that was what he thought was best for his children, he'd stretch every nerve and work himself into the ground to make sure he *could* afford it, but he doesn't want them to grow up feeling isolated, clinging to him as their sole parent. He wants them to experience what living with two opposite-sex adults is like, to participate in the natural give-and-take of family life, to see that adults can quarrel and argue and still want to be with one another and, of course, to grow up with the companionship of their cousins.

"Obviously he tries to keep his overseas and overnight trips as brief as possible, and generally when he is away, the children stay either with us or with Jon and Jenny. When Maddy is up she likes to have them because she feels they are company for her Leo and she doesn't want him growing up a spoiled and lonely—"

"Maddy…?" Tullah queried.

"Yes, my cousin Max's wife. They live in London. Max is a practising barrister with one of, if not the most prestigious sets of London chambers." She pulled a wry face. "He's also not one of my favourite people, I'm afraid, although I shouldn't say that because everyone says how very much like my father he is. Perhaps that's why in a way… Anyway," she continued, briskly catching herself up, "Max is very definitely the apple of Gramps's eye and his favourite and whenever they come home, they always stay with him."

"Doesn't Caspar mind you having Saul's children, Livvy?" Tullah asked her curiously.

"Caspar? No. Why on earth should he?"

Tullah couldn't quite meet her eyes. "Well… after all, you and Saul…"

"Me and Saul nothing," Olivia exploded, shaking her head. "That's the second time you've brought that up. Look, I admit that when Caspar and I first got back together again, he *was* a little bit distant with Saul and saw him as something of a rival. But he soon realised what the real situation was and that Saul and I…well, that we'd both reacted overemotionally to the problems we were having to face and the fact that once, years ago when I was a teenager, I'd had a mammoth crush on Saul, which he wisely had largely ignored at the time. Caspar knows now that Saul's and my relationship was never any threat to my love for him. We're *cousins*, Tullah, that's all," she emphasised, "and my feelings for Saul, my love for him, are that of a cousin. As a matter of fact, he and Caspar have become very close friends," she added with a smile and then demanded, "Now, about dinner on Saturday...?"

"I'd love to come," Tullah accepted.

There was no point in harping on about what she had heard at the wedding about Saul's alleged adultery with Olivia. Olivia, it was obvious, genuinely saw him purely and non-sexually as her cousin. But what about Saul? Did *he* see Olivia in the same way and what about his seduction of Jon and Jenny's teenage daughter?

"I saw the most wonderful house the other day," Tullah confided to her friend ten minutes later as she walked her to her car. "Not that *I* could ever afford anything like it, not unless I won a fortune on the lottery," she said, laughing. "It's at the end of this lane." She nodded in the direction of the track that led past her own cottage. "It's beautiful—an old farmhouse, all mellow bricks and old beams with stone-mullioned windows. It's even got its own small lake. Have you seen it?"

"Er, yes...it is lovely," Olivia agreed. "Actually Tullah..."

"I know." Tullah laughed again. "It most definitely has got potential. And if the owner just happened to be single and halfway presentable, I might just be tempted to make an honest man out of him. Me and half the entire female population of Cheshire into the bargain, no doubt," she added with a rueful smile, but to her surprise Olivia didn't appear to share her amusement.

Tullah frowned to herself as she watched her friend drive away. She hoped she hadn't offended or hurt Olivia with her comments about her relationship with Saul. She certainly hadn't intended to do so, and nor did she want to pry.

So Saul had full custody of his three children. She was still frowning over the rather different light this cast over her view of his personality as she walked back to the cottage.

"Hello, I'm Meg. Who are you?"

Tullah, who had gone upstairs on Olivia's instructions to leave her jacket in Olivia and Caspar's bedroom, paused in some surprise to look down at the small pyjama-clad figure who had suddenly appeared in the open bedroom doorway.

"Hello, Meg, I'm Tullah," she answered. She had always liked children and got on well with them and she had to admit there was something about this little one that would have touched the hardest of adult hearts.

She had her father's attractive, slightly olive skin and a mop of golden brown curls allied to hazel eyes with the thickest eyelashes and the most endearing dimples on either side of her mouth.

But along with the curiosity in her eyes, Tullah could see a faint shadow of apprehension, and remembering what Olivia had said about the little girl's nightmares, she crouched down beside her and asked conversationally, "Shouldn't you be in bed?"

"Well, yes, I should really," Meg admitted, giving her a disarming smile as she explained, "But Aunt Livvy said that a very special friend of hers was coming to dinner and I wanted to see you."

"Ah well, now that you have seen me, I think perhaps you ought to go back to bed, don't you?"

Tullah suggested firmly. "Which bedroom are you sleeping in?"

"This one," Meg told her, slipping her hand into Tullah's hand pointing to one of the other doors leading off the landing. "Will you tuck me up in bed?" she asked. "My daddy always does, but he isn't here. He's had to go away on business in a plane. My mummy lives in America," she added inconsequentially. "*We* went on a plane to see her but I didn't like it. Jem and Robbie didn't like it, either. We didn't like Palmer…that's my mummy's new daddy," she explained misleadingly. But Tullah, with the benefit of Olivia's information about Saul's marriage, knew exactly what she meant. Palmer was, no doubt, the new partner who didn't want to have the children from Hillary's first marriage living with them.

Tullah found it extremely hard to understand why. It would, she suspected, be extremely easy to love the little moppet gazing up at her so trustingly as they walked across the landing together.

When she pushed open the bedroom door Meg had indicated, Tullah realised that she wasn't the only occupant of the large bedroom with its four single beds. The facial features of both the children who lay watching her silently bore a distinctive resemblance to Saul, his elder daughter specifically so, Tullah decided.

As Tullah guided Meg towards the rumpled bed, which was obviously hers, she informed her in a loud whisper, "That bed there is for Amelia when she gets big enough and then the four of us will be together, but she still has to sleep in her cot now."

"She would sleep, you mean, if you didn't keep going in and waking her up," the eldest of the trio grumbled to Meg as she sat upright in bed and studied Tullah.

"I don't wake her," Meg defended herself indignantly. "I just go and look—"

"No, you don't! You were poking her with your fingers, I saw you."

"I was just tickling her. She wanted me to."

"Who are you?" a wary, young male voice asked Tullah as she straightened Meg's bed and held back the covers invitingly so that she could climb in.

"She's Auntie Livvy's special friend," Meg informed her brother before Tullah could say anything. "My daddy always reads us a story when we go to bed. Will you read us one?" she asked Tullah pleadingly, her eyes all melting innocence.

Tullah paused. The other two were still watching her in silence and she could see a small stack of children's books on the bedside table. Olivia had already informed her that her other dinner guests had not yet arrived and that there was nothing she could do to help in the kitchen.

"Well, just a short one," she agreed. "What would you like me to read?"

"This one," Meg announced, diving beneath the bed to retrieve a book Tullah hadn't noticed.

"*Wind in the Willows*?"

"Dad reads us a chapter every night when he's at home."

Tullah turned round from tucking Meg back into bed to smile at her elder sister. "Well, I can't promise to read a whole chapter," she told her. "Can you remember where he got up to?"

"Yes, I can…it's here," she informed Tullah, hopping out of bed to turn the pages for her.

Jemima stood close to Tullah and she felt the thin sharpness of her growing bones and body. Unlike Meg's, her eyes were watchful and wary, her body slightly tense as though she was already preparing herself for a rebuff.

"You'll have to read slowly," she advised Tullah. "Meg is too young to understand all the words yet."

"No, I'm not," Meg argued.

"Yes, you are," Jemima contradicted her flatly. "Dad sometimes has to explain the really big ones even to me," she informed Tullah.

"Well, if I read one you don't understand, then you must stop me and I'll explain it for you," Tullah promised gravely, adding, "Right, are you ready?"

Ten minutes later much to her own amazement, she was as deeply engrossed in the story as the three silently listening children. Meg was sitting up in her bed, round-eyed as she clasped the bedclothes around her, and at some point in the proceedings, both Robert and Jemima had also clambered on to Meg's bed, where Tullah had fulfilled her adult responsibility towards them by insisting that they were to wrap themselves in their quilts to protect them from the cold—not that it was a particularly cold night but still…

When she had reached the end of the chapter, Tullah reluctantly closed the book.

"Oh, can't we have some more?" Meg pleaded.

Tullah shook her head. "I'm afraid not. If I don't

go down soon, Livvy will be coming upstairs to find out where I am."

"Uncle James is coming to dinner, as well," Meg informed her. "He's nice, I like him. Have you got a daddy?" she asked Tullah.

"Er..."

"She doesn't mean that," Jemima informed her. "What she means is are you married? Meg thinks that husbands are daddies."

"Ah...yes, I see." Tullah thanked her gravely. "Well, no, I'm not married, Meg."

"Our mummy and daddy aren't married any more, are they?" she surprised Tullah by telling her as she appealed to her siblings for corroboration of her statement.

"Mum and Dad are divorced," Robert agreed stoically. "Mum lives in America."

"Yes, but *we* live here with Daddy, don't we?" Meg insisted, and Tullah could see the anxiety momentarily shadow all three pairs of matching hazel eyes as she said it.

"My parents are divorced, too," she offered gently, wanting to reassure them.

"And did you live with your daddy?" Meg asked her curiously.

"No, I lived with my mummy, my mother," Tullah explained.

Several minutes earlier she had heard a car drive up and stop and then the front door open. Any second now Olivia would be coming upstairs to see what she was doing. It was time to bring this conversation to a close and remind the children that by rights they ought to be in bed and asleep.

"Our mother didn't want us."

Jemima's stark, almost cold statement made the hairs stand up on the back of Tullah's neck. She could almost feel the tension vibrating from the girl's sharp-boned little body, but as much as she ached to hold her in her arms and comfort her, Tullah reminded herself that she was, after all, a stranger to Saul's children, no matter how much she might empathise with their situation.

"Sometimes adults have to make choices that can…that seem hurtful," she began instead, carefully searching for the right words and yet knowing that in Saul's wife's place, there was no way…no way at all she would ever, ever have put her own sexual needs above the emotional needs of her children.

The bedroom door opened, admitting a strong

beam of light from the landing and a male figure.

"Daddy!" Meg shrieked, struggling excitedly out of bed and launching herself at him.

"What's going on here?" Tullah heard Saul's voice asking mock-sternly as he caught her up in his arms and by some almost magical sleight of hand, or so it appeared to her, managed at the same time to transfer her to one arm whilst he held out the other to hold his other two children equally close.

"Tullah was reading us a story," Meg told him.

"Mmm...so I see, and that was *her* idea, was it?" Saul asked her dryly. "You three should be asleep, not badgering Tullah into reading to you. I'm sorry," he apologised to Tullah.

"I'm not," Tullah responded truthfully. "I enjoyed it."

She had enjoyed it but now she felt distinctly uncomfortable and out of place and something else, as well. Something she wasn't prepared to acknowledge or explore. All she knew was that for some reason, being in this half-shadowed bedroom with Saul whilst he perched on the small bed surrounded by his children made her feel oddly breathless and quivery inside, oddly vulnerable and unfamiliarly emotional as though… as though—

"There you are." Olivia's plaintive voice broke into the too heavy silence. "Dinner is virtually ready."

"I'll take these three off your hands," Saul offered, but Olivia shook her head.

"They might as well stay now and you can have dinner with us. How come you're back so soon anyway?" she questioned as Saul firmly returned the children to their rightful beds and tucked them in with a stern paternal admonition to go to sleep.

"Oh, the meeting was cancelled. It's been rescheduled, so I decided I might as well fly home this evening instead of hanging round Brussels until tomorrow."

"Come down when you're ready," Olivia advised him. "I've got to go and check on something in the kitchen," she explained as she hurried away, leaving Tullah on her own with the children—and Saul.

"Night-night, Daddy," Meg murmured drowsily, lifting her head from her pillow to kiss Saul as he bent over her, and then to Tullah's consternation, she added, "I want Tullah to kiss me, as well."

Uncomfortably Tullah edged carefully round Saul as he turned towards Robert's bed.

"Night-night, Tullah. Thank you for reading to us," Meg told her lovingly as Tullah kissed her gently.

She could feel Saul standing behind her, feel him almost as though their bodies, their skins, were actually touching. Her face flamed at the treacherous direction her thoughts were taking. Not that they had any reason to do so, she decided crossly as she followed Olivia back downstairs five minutes later.

She couldn't even begin to think why her heart had suddenly decided it wanted to audition for a circus act and turn spectacularly dizzying and breathtaking somersaults. It was impossible that such an unfamiliar reaction could have been caused by Saul's proximity. Impossible, unpalatable and completely untenable, she decided firmly and then gasped aloud as her foot missed one of Olivia's uneven stairs and she started to fall forward.

Instinctively she cried out, but Saul was already responding to her plight, quickly reaching out to grasp hold of and virtually swing Tullah off her feet and back against his body as he caught her mid-fall.

Shaken and breathless, Tullah could only cling weakly to him as she later wrathfully berated herself like a second-rate actress trying for a part in *Gone with the Wind*. Only she was no dainty, fragile lightweight but a healthy, modern young woman who prided herself on keeping her rebelliously feminine curves under control with thrice-weekly gym workouts and as many fresh-air walks as she could fit into her busy schedule.

But if the strain of supporting her, *holding* her wrapped against his chest, his *body*, enfolded in his arms, was imposing any kind of physical strain on him, Saul certainly wasn't showing it, Tullah acknowledged.

Yet, his heartbeat *had* accelerated a tad, and his muscles had firmed as his body tautly braced itself against her weight. But from her snugly secure position against his body with her head tucked protectively into the comfortable space between his shoulder and his jaw that might have been made for her, she could neither see nor feel any evidence of his straining against her weight.

"I…I…you can put me down now," Tullah started to tell Saul in what she had intended to be a courteous though dismissively distant tone but what instead sounded revoltingly coy and horridly breathless.

"That's just as well because I'm afraid my endurance and stamina are just about to give in. They aren't really up to much more," Saul informed her dryly.

Feeling mortified, Tullah immediately started to push herself away from him as he carefully set her back down on her own feet. It was perhaps unfair of her to feel that he was being ungallant in announcing that he found her too heavy, but she was, after all, a woman and as such surely allowed to be a little illogical if and when she wished.

"I'm sorry if I'm too heavy," she apologised insincerely once she was back on the floor and able to take a couple of wary steps away from him. She moved a little bit farther downstairs but this time concentrating on where she was putting her feet and holding on to the stair rail in addition.

"I never said you were too heavy," Saul murmured to her before leaning forward and almost absently straightening the rucked collar of her top.

Tullah gaped at him, too caught off guard by

the unconscious intimacy of his careful, almost paternal touch, the kind of touch she could so easily imagine him giving to one of his children, to think to question his words very deeply. If he wanted to pretend to backtrack and pretend that he hadn't implied she was too heavy…

His hand was still resting on her shoulder, his fingertips touching the bare flesh of her collarbone.

Upstairs the children had fallen silent, Olivia was still in the kitchen and the other two men in the sitting room. They were completely alone in the still intimacy of the narrow stairway.

If Saul *hadn't* meant that she was too heavy, then what exactly had he meant?

Tullah turned her head towards him, intending to ask and then didn't, couldn't, as the small action of turning her head dislodged his hand from her shoulder, causing it to lodge in the open neck of her top.

Tullah froze as she felt the warm, hard imprint of Saul's palm and fingertips against her breast and then frantically tried to pull back from it.

To her dismay, she could feel the fabric of her top starting to give, dragged down by the combined weight of Saul's hand and her own movement to expose the upper curve of her breasts. She could hear quite clearly the sound of Saul's indrawn breath as he looked down at her body and she knew that her angry "Let go of me' was uttered just those vital seconds too late. Vital seconds during which she had said nothing, *done* nothing, to reject the presence of Saul's hand against her breast, and even worse, done nothing to stop her own sharp pang of physical response to it.

As he removed his hand from Tullah's body, Saul wondered just what the hell he thought he was doing. He was an adult, damn it, with surely enough control over himself to make sure that those body-aching, teeth-gritting, tantalising mental images he had of Tullah's breasts, of her whole body naked to his touch, to the slow, sensual exploration of his hands and mouth remained just exactly that.

He had *seen* the look of mingled anger and shock she had given him as she stepped back from him just now and he knew perfectly well that the kind of fantasies he was being tormented with at the moment were most definitely not ones she would share.

"Ah, there you are, you two. I was just coming

to look for you," Olivia announced, emerging into the hallway below them.

Quickly Tullah hurried down the remaining stairs uncomfortably conscious of the way her breasts had actually begun to ache as though… As though what? Not as though she had actually wanted Saul to touch her, to caress her.

Of course not. What a totally ridiculous thought. It irked her and added to her existing antipathy towards him that, for whatever reason, his presence should make her feel so acutely aware of herself, of her body, in such a basic and sexual way, the ache in her breasts an uncomfortable reminder of a reaction to him she would much rather have safely dismissed and forgotten.

"Oh, I don't believe you. You couldn't have done any such thing," Tullah protested in between giggles after James had detailed some of the exploits he and his brother and Chester cousins had got up to in their shared youth.

"Oh, that was nothing," James said, grinning at her, "and if you don't believe me, ask Saul. He was the one who was detailed to take charge of us during the long summer holidays."

"Poor Saul, we all used to drive you mad, didn't

we?" Olivia interposed. "I can remember when your parents used to come and stay at Queensmead with Gramps, and the others would come over from Chester and you'd be put in charge of us."

"So can I," Saul agreed feelingly, adding wryly, "I'm surprised I wasn't grey by the time I was eighteen."

As she listened to their good-natured teasing of one another, Tullah was conscious of a small sense of envy. Although she and her sister had been reasonably close and their mother had done her utmost to make sure that her divorce from their father didn't affect them too badly, Tullah had experienced the consequences of it very strongly. Her sister had been at university when it happened and Tullah had felt very much on her own, very alienated, and it was hard not to feel just that little bit envious of Olivia and her cousins, of their camaraderie, their sense of belonging; of their unity; of the family history they so clearly shared, of the very obvious knowledge that no matter how often they might quarrel, no matter what their differences, nothing could ever break the bonds of family that bound them to one another.

"I can remember when you taught us to fish," she heard James reminiscing to Saul.

"So can I," Saul agreed grimly, "especially that time you ignored me when I told you to let me take the line and you fell in."

"You made us all go back to Queensmead and you were trying to dry him off in front of the Aga when Aunt Ruth came in. We all thought she was going to be cross but she just looked at us and then told James to go upstairs and have a hot bath and get some dry clothes on."

"And then the very next day she took us all swimming and arranged for us to have life-saving lessons."

"When I think about it, it is a wonder we *didn't* turn your hair grey, Saul, or that you didn't try to drown us all in exasperation, at the very least."

"Don't think I wasn't ever tempted," Saul responded dryly.

Tullah couldn't remember when she had enjoyed an evening so much and she said so to Olivia later when the two of them relaxed over a cup of coffee whilst the men washed up.

"James is terrific fun," she added warmly.

"Yes, he is, isn't he?" Olivia agreed with a satisfied smile. "I thought you'd like him. You must take him up on his offer to show you round the castle at Chester. It isn't long ago that prisoners were still kept there and it has a fascinating history."

"He was telling me that he specialises in medical compensation claims."

"Yes, he does. Although you might not guess it from listening to him tonight. He really is a first-rate prosecutor. Of the two of them you'd think Luke would be the one who excelled at that, but Luke actually prefers to defend, which reminds me, I must give Bobbie a ring. She's dying to meet you."

Tullah looked surprised.

"Her own family background is in the law," Olivia explained. "On her father's side, although he is actually a politician, and as Bobbie says, much as she wants to spend these early years at home with Francesca, she does miss the faster pace of her old professional life. Jon and I are hoping to persuade her to join us on a part-time basis in the Haslewich law practice if we can."

As the men returned from the kitchen, Tullah glanced at her watch and was shocked to discover how late it was. "Heavens, I must go," she announced, finishing her coffee and standing up. "I hadn't realised it was that time…."

"Look, why don't you leave your car here and let James run you home?" Olivia suggested as she watched Tullah stifle a yawn. "You could always come back for it in the morning."

It was a tempting suggestion, not the least because she had enjoyed James's company so much over dinner, but just as she was wavering about it, Tullah happened to catch a glimpse of Saul out of the corner of her eye. He was frowning slightly as though he did not find Olivia's idea particularly appealing.

Because he was staying overnight and that would mean when she returned to collect her car that he would have to see her?

Just what kind of woman did he think she was? The kind who just because a man made the instinctive gesture of preventing her from falling down a flight of stairs, automatically and stupidly assumed that his interest in her was personal and sexual. How ridiculous and how typical of the man she knew him to be. Vanity and self-conceit went hand in hand with men of his type. She should know.

And no, of course she wasn't deliberately

winding herself up into a state of defensive antipathy towards Saul. Why should she need to? She was *already* antipathetic towards him; there was no need for her to feel she had to manufacture such a state of mind, or to cling defensively to it once she had.

"No, there's really no need," she assured James firmly as he started to reiterate Olivia's offer.

"Pity," he teased, only half-joking as he clasped rather than shook her hand in farewell.

To Saul she did very little more than offer the merest tip of her fingers, her expression coolly dismissive as she deliberately kept as much physical distance between them as she could, which made it all the more irritating and ridiculous when, as she settled herself into her car five minutes later, it was the hard warmth of Saul's body against hers as he rescued her from her near mishap her body remembered—that and the sense of security and pleasure that had gone with it and with being so close to him.

CHAPTER SIX

YUCK… When autumn came she must remember to get someone in to prune the pretty sycamore tree that had been in full bloom at the side of the cottage when she first saw it, but that had also filled in her gutters with dead leaves over the years. That was why she was perching on top of the ladder she had gone out and bought for herself earlier that morning for the specific purpose of cleaning her gutters of leaves so that the rainwater would keep off the cottage's exterior walls.

Dressed in a pair of jeans and a T-shirt plus a pair of heavy-duty protective gloves, she had climbed the ladder initially with some trepidation but had quickly discovered that so long as she refrained from moving too quickly and looking down, her self-imposed task kept her too busy to worry about being so far off the ground.

"Aha! Gotcha!" she exclaimed with relish as she discovered a particularly thick clump of leaves and debris blocking the full width of the gutter. No wonder there were traces of damp on the spare bedroom wall.

Happily engaged in her task, Tullah was only vaguely aware of the car coming up the lane and even when she heard it stop she simply assumed that whoever was driving it was calling on her next-door neighbours.

It wasn't until she heard little Meg's familiar voice that she realised she was wrong.

Assuming that Olivia must have decided to call on her and bring the children with her, she called out cheerfully, "Hang on, I'm coming down," and proceeded to back carefully down the ladder.

"Daddy, Daddy, come and look at Tullah!"

Daddy!

Saul was with the children!

Immediately Tullah swung round to look and then wished she hadn't. If she was honest, she had never felt particularly comfortable with heights or ladders and it was only her strong-minded determination to be independent that had enabled her to get up this ladder in the first place. But now, the shock of discovering Saul frowning up at her, combined with the queasy, unpleasant and dizzying realisation that she was still only half-way down the ladder, made her suddenly lose her nerve, while her eyes widened with distress as she clung on tightly.

"Don't look down," she heard Saul instructing her irritably as he correctly interpreted the expression on her face. "*No! Don't* look down," he repeated even more bitingly as she ignored his instruction and lifted one shaking hand to her forehead as she tried to fight back her dizziness.

It was the wrong thing to do. Tullah heard both Jemima and Meg gasp, their small faces paling as they looked up towards her.

"Tullah, put both hands on the ladder. Climb down slowly," she heard Saul directing her.

Tullah swallowed hard. She could *hear* what he was saying; she *knew* what she was supposed to do. For heaven's sake, she could *see* for herself what she *should* do, but for some totally incomprehensible reason she simply could not do it. There was no way she could walk backwards down the ladder…no way at all. And so, instead, she tried to turn round and then froze as Saul let out what sounded like a maddened roar of rage.

"No! No! *No*! Stay where you are!"

Stay where you are. Couldn't the stupid man see that that was exactly what she was trying to do…that the last thing she had any intention of wanting to do was to go anywhere? If only she could simply close her eyes and wish herself back on the ground, then that was exactly what she *would* do because there was no way…no way at all she could climb the rest of the way down this horrid, rickety, unsafe ladder that wobbled perilously with every breath she took. And if, *if* she ever got back safely down to earth, the first thing…well, the first thing she intended to do was let the DIY store know just what she thought of their supposedly foolproof and completely safe ladder. The very last thing it felt like right now was safe; the very last thing *she* felt like was safe….

"Hurry up, Daddy, she's going to fall," she heard a breathless Meg exclaiming anxiously.

Beside her Robert chimed in disgust, "Girls…"

Weakly Tullah closed her eyes. She felt safer that way. At least then she couldn't *see* the ground wavering all those many, many feet below her, nor could she see the ladder moving from side to side even if she could still feel it, but best of all, with her eyes closed, she couldn't see Saul's wrathful face!

"Let go of the ladder, Tullah. *Let* go of the ladder."

Try as she might, Tullah couldn't respond to Saul's terse command, not even with him standing four-square on the ladder just below her, facing the right way, of course.

"Look, all you have to do is let go of the ladder and turn round and then I'll guide you down. It couldn't be simpler."

"I…I can't," Tullah admitted huskily. "I *can't* let go." And as for turning round… She gave a small shudder, tensing as Saul took another step up towards her, convinced that the ladder couldn't bear both their weights and terrified that it might somehow start to slide and that they would both be thrown to the ground and suffer heaven alone knew what injuries.

Beneath his breath Saul cursed and then before Tullah could guess what he intended to do, he reached upwards, somehow managing to balance himself on the ladder whilst he prised both her hands free of its support. As she started to panic, he commanded, "Keep still, you stupid creature, otherwise you'll have the pair of us falling," before neatly toppling her over his shoulder in a classic fireman's-lift fashion and then, as she gasped for breath and closed her eyes, starting to climb back down the ladder.

"Tullah, you looked ever so funny," Meg said with a giggle when Saul finally reached the ground with his burden and set her on her feet, adding to her father, "You are clever, Daddy, rescuing her like that."

Rescuing her? Tullah's eyes flashed indignant, defensive sparks as she lifted her head and tossed her hair back over her shoulders. At some point in the proceedings, it had come free of its confining hair band and was now hanging in a tousled mass of curls all over the place.

"I wouldn't have *needed* rescuing if you hadn't frightened me to death calling out to me like that," she accused Saul defensively. "I was doing fine until you came along."

"Were you?" Saul asked her dryly. "Tell me something, how many times have you actually climbed up a full house-height ladder before, Tullah?"

"Er, I managed to climb up it without any problems," she informed him haughtily.

"Climbing up a ladder is the easy bit," Robert informed her unnecessarily. "It's climbing down again that's the hard bit."

"Thank you, Robert, but I think that Tullah has already demonstrated that fact to us," Saul intervened calmly. Then turning towards Tullah so that the children couldn't quite hear what he was saying, he added in a soft undertone, "If I were a different kind of man, I might find it rather flattering that you're prepared to go to such dangerous lengths to fling yourself into my arms, Tullah, but if you really want to be there..."

"I don't!" Tullah responded with vehement antagonism while being careful to ensure that her words didn't reach the children. She ignored both the amusement curling his mouth and the open invitation in the good humour lightening his eyes to participate in the tension-breaking joke he was trying to share with her. "In *your* arms is the very last place I want to be," she responded acidly, "and you are the very last man I'd—"

"Be careful, Tullah," Saul interrupted her curtly, "otherwise..."

"Otherwise what?" she muttered furiously. "Otherwise you might just think I'm offering you some kind of sexual challenge, because that's the kind of man you are, isn't it? The kind that derives some sort of sick pleasure from adding another female scalp to his belt, the kind—"

"My God," Saul breathed, all the earlier good humour dying out of his face to be replaced by a look of hard contempt. "The man who takes you on really will have a problem on his hands. But I'll tell you something for nothing, Tullah. There's absolutely no way that man would *ever* be me. For a start—"

"For a start, I'm not your type," Tullah flung at him gratingly, her lip curling. "No, *you* prefer to pick on the naïve and vulnerable, don't you? Girls too young to know what you really are…."

Tullah was literally shaking with emotion as she hurled the words at him like blows, too caught up in the intensity of her feelings to be aware that the children might sense, if not actually hear, the bitterness of their low-voiced exchange until she heard Meg demanding in a slightly quavery voice, "Daddy…"

Saul reacted immediately, forcing his mouth into a smile as he turned towards his youngest child, his voice softening as he knelt down and picked her up.

To her own confusion and horror, Tullah felt a huge lump rise in her throat and her eyes begin to film with tears as she recognised the urgency and intensity with which he responded to Meg's need.

There, at least, he *was* different from her father and from the man who had betrayed her adoring, youthful, immature love and she couldn't deny it, not with the evidence of his care and concern for his children in front of her eyes.

Over Meg's down-bent head as she nestled in his arms, Saul's glance met Tullah's and she flinched from his cold contempt.

Jemima and Robert had moved closer to their father, flanking him almost protectively. Tullah swallowed. "It was very nice of your daddy to bring you to see me—" she began.

"Daddy didn't bring us to see you' Jemima interrupted her. "We were on our way home when we saw you up the ladder. Daddy didn't think you looked safe."

On their way *home*. Tullah frowned as she looked down the lane that led past her cottage. It only went to one house, the house she had described to Olivia not so very long ago as being her dream home.

Saul lived there!

"I'm sorry I delayed you," she finally managed

to say, her voice stiff as she carefully avoided meeting Saul's face.

"You will come and see us some time, won't you?" Meg coaxed as she wriggled out of Saul's arms and came over to Tullah, resting her hand invitingly on Tullah's arm. "I'd like you to read me some more stories and you can play with my new Barbie if you like...she's got lots of clothes and her own car and..."

Behind Meg, Jemima made a small sound of sisterly disgust.

Warily Tullah watched as Saul instructed them to say their goodbyes and then started to shepherd them back to his car.

The ladder was still leaning against the house. Tullah eyed it with disfavour. "It's all your fault," she scolded it firmly. "If it hadn't been for you..."

Throw herself into his arms indeed. As if she would. Why, she would rather...she would rather...she'd rather throw herself into a pit of snakes, she decided fiercely and untruthfully.

"Oh, and by the way, I've got a bone to pick with you."

"Have you, where? I thought you'd put them all

in this stock you're making," Olivia commented facetiously as she watched Tullah frowning over the stock she was rendering down from some chicken carcass. "What are you going to use this for, by the way?" she enquired thoughtfully. But if she had hoped to divert Tullah from the real object of her conversation, she was mistaken.

"Home-made chicken and leek soup," Tullah informed her briefly before continuing, "You might have told me when I was going on about the house up the road that it belonged to Saul."

"Ah...well... Chicken and leek—that's one of my favourites."

"Well, it isn't made yet and it never will be if you don't stop distracting me," Tullah warned her.

"Um...knowing how you feel about Saul I thought you might be embarrassed if I told you that the house you'd been raving about living in belonged to him."

"Not half as embarrassed as I was to discover that he wasn't bringing the children to visit me as I'd assumed, but quite the contrary, was merely on his way home," Tullah told her feelingly.

"Forget about Saul," Olivia urged, "and tell me what you thought of James."

Forget about him! If only she could. Olivia couldn't know just how much she wanted to comply with her request.

"James? I liked him," she told Olivia truthfully. "He's fun."

"You liked him. I knew you would," Olivia pounced. "You should invite him round for a meal. Men like home cooking."

Tullah gave her a suspicious look. "*I* like home cooking," she informed her pointedly, "which is why I'm making myself some home-made soup."

"Well, there's going to be more than enough here for one person. Eating by yourself is lonely. Eating with someone else is much more fun," Olivia wheedled winningly.

"But I shan't *be* eating by myself," Tullah informed her, hiding a grin.

"You've already invited James over for dinner…? *Why* didn't you say so?" Olivia demanded excitedly.

"Not James. Mary and Ivy from next door," Tullah corrected her.

Olivia gave her a wry look, "But James *has* been in touch," Olivia guessed.

"Yes, he has," Tullah agreed repressively and

then gave in and admitted, "I'm meeting him for a drink on Wednesday."

"I knew the two of you would get on," Olivia said, grinning.

"He's good fun. I like him," Tullah agreed, adding pointedly, "but *only* as a friend."

"Of course," Olivia agreed meekly.

"Mary and Ivy should be good company, too. They're very interesting to listen to. They know so much about the history of the area. I hadn't realised, for instance, that the site of Aarlston's new complex was originally a battlefield."

"During the Civil War, yes, it was," Olivia affirmed. "Haslewich was a very strategic site in those times, standing as it does on the crossroads of the two main access routes north and south and east and west. In Roman times all the salt mined locally was transported by mules through Haslewich to Chester and from there shipped overseas. The "'wich' in Haslewich comes from a word that originally meant salt-works and it was the salt that initially made the area so valuable and rich."

"Thanks for the history lesson," Tullah teased her.

"Well, the town *does* have a very interesting

history," Olivia defended her native hearth, "and it's still making history now in the way it's becoming a centre for modern business and modern technology. How are you liking your new job, by the way?" she asked Tullah, changing the subject.

"I'm loving it," Tullah told her truthfully. "Whether it's a facet of the company or whether it's because we're country and not city based, I don't know, but there's definitely a very good working atmosphere in the department, a true feeling of being part of a team, a sense of cooperation and genuine willingness to be open and helpful to co-workers."

"Mmm...well, they do say that in any business the atmosphere of the place and the attitudes of the workers are often a reflection of the man or woman at the top, and Saul *does* have the reputation of being able to bring out the best in those who work under him, of being able to motivate them and give them a feeling of self-worth and value."

"Hmm...I've hardly seen Saul, and from what I've heard, he doesn't spend an awful lot of time in the office," Tullah told her semi-disparagingly.

"Maybe not, but I'll bet you he still has his

finger on the pulse of the operation and knows exactly what's going on, and as for being away a lot..." She frowned. "Maybe he is at the moment but that can only be a temporary thing. After all, the main reason he transferred to the European side is because he wants to spend more time at home with the children."

Tullah digested her comments in silence. Much as she may have wanted to cling to her initial belief that Saul was an absent and uncaring father, she was forced to acknowledge that it simply wasn't true.

She might also wilfully and stubbornly want to cling to the conviction that Saul had somehow or other used his legal knowledge and expertise to unfairly win custody of the children away from his wife, but honesty compelled her to admit that this wasn't so.

The children were with Saul not because he had been determined to win custody of them for any malicious or ego boosting purpose, but purely and simply because the court had acknowledged that that was what the children wanted, what Saul's wife wanted and what it deemed was in the children's best interests.

So what! Saul might be the world's best father,

but that didn't alter the fact that he *had* tried to seduce Olivia and was now making a play for her not quite yet twenty-year-old cousin. A girl probably young enough to be his daughter and a girl, moreover, who was closely related to him.

And Saul was a man who was powerfully charismatic enough, sensual enough, *male* enough, indeed *more* than male enough, to make her own heart beat faster and her own body react to him, never mind that of a naïve, inexperienced girl.

"I must say, I'm looking forward to this Masquerade Ball Aarlston's holding," Olivia commented. "It sounds as though it's very definitely going to be *the* summer event for the county. I understand they're holding it in the grounds of Fitzburgh Place."

"Yes. I know," Tullah affirmed. "Apparently they're going to re-create the kind of event they used to hold in London in the eighteenth century, complete with a quartet playing Handel and gondolas on the ornamental canal and lake. Everyone has to wear eighteenth-century costumes and be masked. The buffet will be copied from the menu for an eighteenth-century wedding feast and the finale of the evening is to be a spectacular fireworks display."

"Mmm...it promises to be quite something. All Aarlston's employees are being invited plus half the town from what I've heard, and all of the local landed gentry, including the Lord Lieutenant of the county. Actually, Bobbie mentioned it the other day and suggested that we might make an "'all girls' trip to London to sort out our costumes.

"We could stay overnight and take in a show," Olivia enthused, warming to her theme. "I can't wait to see myself dressed up or rather, in my case, trussed up *à la Dangerous Liaisons*. Not that any of us will be able to hold a candle to you," she added mournfully whilst Tullah was still laughing. "You've got the perfect figure for that kind of dress, all luscious curves and a tiny little waist."

"Pity, then, that I'm living in the twentieth century and not the eighteenth," Tullah remarked dryly.

"Your kind of figure *never* goes out of fashion," Olivia informed her firmly.

"A couple of days in London would be fun," Tullah allowed. "When were you thinking of going?"

"That depends. I'm not sure yet but I'll let you know."

* * *

"Are you sure I can't persuade you to have another drink?" James urged Tullah.

Tullah shook her head firmly and explained, "I'm really going to have to go because I've got some work to do this evening."

"Pity," James sighed. "I was hoping to persuade you to have supper with me. Perhaps another time…"

Tullah smiled.

She had been pleased when James had telephoned and suggested they meet up early on the Wednesday evening for a drink and she had enjoyed seeing him again, but the wine bar he had nominated as their meeting place was beginning to fill up and she had spoken the truth when she told him that she had work waiting for her at home.

"Well, at least allow me to walk you to your car," James offered as Tullah climbed off her stool and started to make her way through the now very crowded wine bar towards the exit. "Good heavens, here's Saul," James told her, calling out to the other man to attract his attention before Tullah could protest.

Saul appeared to be on his own and, from the way he was frowning, no more pleased to see her than she was him, Tullah admitted as she watched him make his way towards them. It only added to her irritation to notice that the crowd, which was presently jostling her quite uncomfortably, parted easily to allow Saul through, one of the women who was part of a group that had rather noisily taken over most of the place, including Tullah's personal space, giving Saul an openly admiring and sexually inviting smile as he walked past her.

"We're just leaving," she heard James telling Saul cheerfully. "I tried to persuade Tullah to have another drink but it seems she's got other plans for the evening."

"I see," Saul said politely but Tullah noticed the way he looked coldly at her. "Well, I wish you both a very pleasant evening," he added formally.

"Well, mine certainly doesn't look like being," James announced good-naturedly, "not now that Tullah has turned down my offer of supper in favour of spending her evening working at home."

"You're going home to *work*?" Saul demanded sharply.

Why was he looking at her like that? Tullah

wondered warily. What was he thinking…that she wasn't up to the job if she needed to put extra time in at home?

"There are some aspects of certain things we're dealing with that I wanted to focus on a bit more," Tullah responded defensively.

"She's obviously a very dedicated employee, Saul," James told him with a wry smile, "unfortunately for me. But you won't get away so easily next time," he warned Tullah teasingly. "Then it will be the full works. A long, leisurely dinner and then—"

"If you're having problems with your work…" Saul overrode James to question Tullah sternly.

"There is *no* problem," Tullah denied sharply. "I simply find it easier to absorb complicated facts away from other distractions."

Behind her, the noisy crowd at the bar swelled to include some latecomers, one of whom stepped back jolting Tullah so that she had to put out a protective hand to stop herself from lurching forward. Only she hadn't bargained for Saul moving at the same time so that instead of preserving the distance between them, her hand ended up palm flat against Saul's body with so little distance between them that when he took a deep breath her breasts were actually pressing against his chest.

Hot-cheeked, Tullah stepped smartly back from him, saying quickly to James, "I *really* must go. No, there's no need to see me to my car. It's daylight after all and you and Saul probably have things to talk about." She touched his arm briefly and then before James could say anything, she took advantage of the momentary gap that appeared in the crowd and dived into it, making her way determinedly towards the exit without daring to look back.

"How well exactly do you and Tullah know one another?" Saul asked James crisply once she had gone.

"Nothing near as well as I'd like to," James admitted ruefully, adding, "Can I get you a drink?"

"No thanks," Saul returned, glancing at his watch as he informed him, "I've got a meeting at the Grosvenor in five minutes."

"The Grosvenor?" James frowned. "Then *what* are you doing in here?"

"I thought I saw someone I knew," Saul replied with deliberate vagueness. It was, after all, true.

He *had* seen James and Tullah and, on seeing them together, had reacted instinctively and in a way he had no intention of discussing with his relative.

In a way, in fact, that left him feeling uneasily aware that perhaps he was not quite so mature as he had fondly imagined.

CHAPTER SEVEN

OLIVIA might think that a curvaceous womanly body never went out of fashion, but fashion designers didn't seem to agree with her, Tullah fumed wrathfully as she tightened the belt to the trousers she was wearing an extra notch.

Lengthwise and on her hips the soft, pure wool creamy beige trousers might fit perfectly but when it came to her waist... She groaned as she realised that even fastened on the very tightest notch the belt was still slipping off her waist. The trouble was that even though she had had the trousers altered when she bought them, she had lost weight since, mainly due to the very natural stress and tension of the moves both of job and home. The problem was that when she *did* lose weight, it always seemed to be around her midsection, giving her a figure that she thought ruefully had a tendency to look more Dolly Parton than an elegant catwalk model.

But there wasn't time for her to get changed into

anything else now; if she didn't leave for work soon, she was going to be late. At least her suit jacket disguised the fact that the trousers were loose around her waist.

What she had said to Olivia about the fact that she was loving her new job was perfectly correct. She even found that she was humming some mornings as she drove into work, a vast difference to the way she had felt in her last months at her old job.

"...bit of a panic this morning," Barbara was informing her half an hour later as she sat down at her desk. "Derek has gone down with this stomach virus that's going round and he was due to fly out to The Hague this morning with the boss."

Tullah frowned as she listened to her. Derek was her own immediate section leader and only the previous night she had worked late to help him put the final touches to the documents he had wanted for the trip to The Hague.

"Someone will have to go in his place," Tullah commented unnecessarily. "It's too late to delay the hearing now."

"Yes, I know," Barbara agreed, rolling her eyes and giving a mock-lascivious smile as she added,

"Pity it isn't going to be me. I wouldn't mind a couple of nights away with our sexy boss."

Tullah raised her eyebrows but said nothing, concentrating instead on the screen she had just switched on.

The internal telephone beside her computer buzzed. She picked it up without taking her eyes off the screen and said automatically, "Tullah Richards."

"Ah, Tullah…good…can you come up to my office, please?"

"Yes, of course."

Tullah was still looking at the screen as she replaced her receiver but she wasn't concentrating on it any longer.

What did Saul want her for?

As she got to her feet and made her way through the office to the lifts, she was mentally reviewing all the work that had passed through her hands in the time she had been with the company. So far as she knew there was nothing there for Saul to find fault with. In fact, only last night as they worked together, Derek had commented on how pleased he was, not just with her work but with the quick way she picked up on and followed through with things.

It wasn't just the lift that was making her stomach muscles protest a little nervously as she stepped out of it and walked down the corridor that led to Saul's office.

When she opened the outer office door, Marsha, gave her a brief smile and told her to go straight in.

Saul was on the telephone when she opened the door. He frowned as he saw her and gestured to her to sit down. He was dressed formally in a dark business suit although he had removed its jacket and loosened the knot of the elegantly patterned tie he was wearing.

"Well, it's very flattering of you to say so, Travis, but I can assure you that Thierry is well qualified to take over from me. In fact, he actually did a postgrad course at Harvard Law School, specialising in international law, which, I'm bound to admit, is more than I ever did."

There was a brief pause whilst the man on the other end of the line started to speak again, and even without trying Tullah could hear the transatlantic voice complaining that no amount of law degrees could match the skills of someone who actually had hands-on experience.

"I appreciate what you're saying, Travis," Saul

interrupted him, "but I reiterate that Thierry is more than up to the job. Just give him time...

"I'm sorry about that," Saul told Tullah briefly when he had finally terminated the call.

Tullah waited in silence, half-expecting, given what she knew about his ego and his vanity, that he would make some comment about the fact that the American on the other end of the line obviously wasn't happy with the French colleague who had been promoted to take over Saul's previous post as deputy head of the corporation's international legal section.

A little to her surprise he made no reference whatsoever to it and instead asked her with a small frown, "You'll have heard that Derek has had to take sick leave?"

"Yes," Tullah replied.

"I understand that you were working very closely with him on this claim against our patent rights we've got pending. The case is due to come up for hearing in court first thing tomorrow morning in The Hague."

"Yes, I was. Derek asked me to research the history of the corporation's rights over the patent, how it was acquired and under what terms the corporation bought it from the first wife of the original patent holder who had obtained it as part of a divorce settlement. It was one of the first patents the corporation purchased virtually twenty years ago now."

"And you're quite definite about the fact that it was originally a twenty-five-year patent?"

"Yes, there's no doubt whatsoever about that, although I did have a rather difficult time tracking down the original records for the patent," Tullah informed him. "The whole case being brought against us rests on the fact that the original patent holder's second wife's family claims that the original patent life was only ten years and not twenty-five and that all royalties and income earned from the patent during the contested years should, by rights, have reverted to them."

"They claim they have a patent document to prove that the patent *was* only for ten years," Saul warned Tullah, frowning again.

"I know. I appreciate that. The case is a very complex and intricate one, quite fascinating from a purely legal point of view, but what I suspect must have happened was that originally the patent *was* registered for ten years and then Gerard Lebruck, the originator of the patent, changed his mind and altered it to twenty-five years but without bothering to destroy the original document. In those days the patent laws weren't as complicated and closely monitored as they are now, of course, and while I'm sure that the Lebruck family believe the patent document they hold to be genuine, in actual fact it isn't."

"Mmm...well, you certainly seem to have all the facts at your fingertips, which is just as well." Saul glanced at his watch. "There isn't going to be enough time to brief anyone else to take Derek's place now, so I'm afraid you're going to have to stand in for him."

"Me? But—"

"Our flight leaves in three hours, which just about gives you time to get home and pack an overnight bag," Saul continued. "Marsha's organising a car and driver to take you home to collect what you need and then drive you straight to the airport. I'll meet you there. Oh, and it might be an idea if you pack something fairly formal.

"Claus van der Laurens who founded the company has retired now, of course, but he still lives in The Hague and takes a very keen interest in the corporation. Most of the shares are still family owned, as you know, and I suspect he'll want to take us both out to dinner after the case."

Her thoughts in confused chaos, Tullah stared at him. It was one thing to sound positive and assertive when confirming the corporation's claim to a twenty-five-year patent to Saul, but to go into court and do the same thing…

Her heart started to beat nervously fast. What if she should fail? What if she should lose the corporation its case *and* its patent, one of the *first* patents on which the corporation's modern-day success had been built. "I don't think…" she began falteringly, but once again Saul overruled her.

"No arguments Tullah," he reminded her tersely. "I want you at the airport in three hours' time to catch that flight."

Her plain black suit teamed with a heavy cream silk shirt should be formal enough for the court hearing, Tullah decided feverishly as she started to pack. She would have to travel in the outfit she was wearing; there simply wasn't going to be time for her to change and to run through her file before she left.

A second shirt, added just in case anything happened to the first one or the court case was extended, joined the other clothes she had already packed. A pair of soft, dull bronze satin trousers and a deceptively demure cream halter-necked top, which buttoned up to the throat at the front but plunged almost to her waist at the back but which could fortunately be covered by the toning bronze lurex-knit jacket she wore over it, were the only things she could think of that would be suitable for dinner with the company's founder. In her previous job, she had attended any number of corporate lunches and had the power suits to prove it, but dressy evening affairs were not really something her wardrobe was equipped to cover.

Undies, make-up, a pair of jeans and a casual top just in case she got the opportunity to tour any of the city's museums and that was about the limit of what she could comfortably fit into the solitary piece of hand luggage Saul had advised her to take with her.

"It will save us having to wait for them to unload the luggage at the other end," he had informed her. "Derek didn't have time to brief me quite as fully as I would have liked before he went off sick and there are a couple of points I want to run through with you."

It would have to be, of course, that her first high-profile task in her new job, her first chance to prove herself, would have to be conducted under Saul's antagonistic eyes. And there was no doubt about it—he was antagonistic towards her. Not to the extent that she would have any cause for complaint and certainly he was always meticulously cool and polite in his dealings on the rare occasions when he crossed her path at work, but nevertheless she knew, and she also, of course, knew why.

Undoubtedly there were those who would say that it was her own fault; that a little judicious forethought and perhaps a little deliberate flattery could have put a very different outlook on things indeed, but that simply wasn't Tullah's way. It never had been and it never would be and most especially it never would be where Saul Crighton was concerned.

But that was getting away from the fact that he was her boss and that, as such, she was professionally bound to pay heed to him and to his demands, at least in so far as her work was concerned.

She gave a small shiver as she finished packing. The cottage still felt slightly cold and damp despite the new central heating system she had had installed. The heating firm had told her that this was because of the thickness of the cottage's walls. There had been some problems installing the new heating system she had been told was a must. As she hurried downstairs to the waiting car and driver, she hoped that the rather damp and dull weather they had been having would change to something much warmer before the date of the corporation's Masquerade Ball.

The news that all the corporation's local employees were going to be invited to the Masquerade Ball had generated a tremendous amount of excitement and eager anticipation and the event certainly promised to be breathtakingly spectacular.

Lord Astlegh, the owner of Fitzburgh Place, with its Italian Renaissance-style gardens designed, so family history had it, by a student of Vanburgh, was being paid a princely sum by the corporation for its use of his exclusive and justly fabled gardens.

"It's because of the man-made canals that lead down to the ornamental lake that they've chosen Fitzburgh Place," Olivia had told Tullah knowledgeably. "Saul was telling us that the managing director of the local division feels it will be a complement to the corporation's original Dutch origins to incorporate a canal theme."

"Amsterdam meets Venice meets Mardi Gras," Tullah had murmured with a grin whilst Olivia had laughed.

She didn't feel very much like smiling now though, Tullah admitted hollowly as the driver warned her that they would soon be approaching the airport.

"I've organised new tickets for you," Marsha had advised Tullah just before she left the office, "but you'll have to pick them up from the airline's desk at the airport, I'm afraid."

Because they were travelling first class, Marsha had also advised Tullah that she did not need to arrive the normal two hours ahead of her flight to check in but merely forty-five minutes instead, but as she waited whilst the clerk shuffled through the papers on her desk for a second time, apparently unable to find any trace of her ticket, Tullah felt her stomach muscles start to cramp with anxiety.

"I want you on that flight," Saul had told her and he certainly hadn't meant it as any kind of compliment.

He would be furious with her if for any reason she didn't make it…for *any* reason.

"I'm sorry," the clerk said reluctantly, "but I'm afraid we don't seem to have a ticket for you."

"No...no ticket...?" What on earth was she supposed to do? Tullah looked round desperately for a phone and then to her relief she saw Saul walking purposefully towards her.

To her *relief*! She didn't have time to examine the way her anxiety fell away from her or her automatic, deep-rooted sense of knowing that Saul would sort everything out, that for him the clerk would somehow or other produce a ticket, out of thin air, Tullah suspected, if necessary.

"Ah, Tullah, good."

"They can't find my ticket," Tullah almost gabbled. "Marsha told me to collect it from the airline desk, but they say they don't have one for me."

"No, that's right. I picked it up earlier when I arrived," Saul told her easily.

"*You* picked it up?" Carefully spacing out the words, Tullah fought to control her rising fury. "*You* picked up *my* ticket?" she reiterated, biting off the syllables, snapping sharply at the words as she tried to swallow her anger by subjecting them to the savage punishment she would have preferred to have inflicted on Saul.

Didn't he *realise* what he had just put her through?

"Is something wrong?" she heard Saul asking her, a small frown creasing the space between his eyebrows as he reached out and placed his hand on her shoulder.

Angrily Tullah shrugged him away and moved back out of range and out of earshot of the curious clerk who was watching them.

"Yes. There *is* something wrong," she hissed at him. "It didn't occur to you, I suppose, that the fact you had collected my ticket might have caused *me* to miss the flight—a flight that you, by the way, had already warned me I had to be on, virtually on pain of death. The clerk told me that there was no ticket for me," she informed him, her voice starting to shake betrayingly.

"Of course there was a ticket for you," Saul asserted. "I—"

"You collected it. Yes, I *know* that *now*...but I didn't know it ten minutes ago when I was wondering what the hell was going on and just how I was going to make that flight without it, did I?"

Saul looked at her thoughtfully and rather gravely. "I understand what you're saying," he told her, "but I think you're overreacting. I *had* intended to be down here to meet you when you arrived, but there was a call for me, which I had to take."

"From Louise, no doubt," Tullah interjected with venomous sweetness, too tightly enmeshed in the panic-induced anger that was the after-effect of her fear that she might miss the flight to even think of monitoring her words or to pause and take stock before crossing the line that divided their professional relationship from her rather more intimate knowledge of Saul's private life.

"Louise?" Saul demanded sharply, his eyes narrowing as he studied her flushed face and stubbornly set mouth. "No, it wasn't from Louise," he told her in a voice so ice-cold that it almost raised blisters on her skin. "As a matter of fact, it was from Jemima. She was in a bit of a panic because she couldn't find Bear."

"Bear?" Tullah repeated. Now that the shock had started to wear off and with it the adrenalin-fuelled burst of anger, she was beginning to feel slightly sick and shaky.

What on earth had got into her? By nature she was inclined to be intense, too much so occasionally perhaps, but she had *never* ever before experienced such a fierce and uncontrollable flash-flood of out-of-control emotion in a professional setting before.

"Bear," Saul affirmed, explaining tersely, "We…*I* gave him to Jemima when she was little and she…" He paused. "She's just getting to the age when she feels very self-conscious about clinging to what she now believes is a childish need for the bedtime comfort of a favourite toy. But when she woke up this morning, she couldn't find Bear and she was panicking a bit, knowing that I wouldn't be there this evening."

Tullah bit her lip, only too easily able to visualise Jemima's feelings. Not for the world would she admit this to anyone, but after her parents' divorce she had derived immense comfort from taking her old battered panda to bed with her. He had become something of a good-luck mascot to her, which was why right now instead of lying comfortably on her bed at home, he was squashed up inside her hand luggage.

Tomorrow's court hearing wasn't the first time she had appeared in court by any means, but it *was* the first time in her new job and it was the first time under the eagle and, she knew, critical eye of Saul Crighton.

There was no way *she* could be his preferred

choice for the task; it was simply that he had no alternative. She was the only one with the necessary information at her fingertips.

Only *she* knew how much of her anxiety over the apparently missing ticket had been generated by her apprehension about what lay ahead. But, of course, she couldn't admit that to Saul.

"Look, it's time we were checking in. Have you got everything?"

"I will have when you give me my ticket," Tullah told him pointedly.

The short flight was smooth and a car and driver were waiting for them at the other end to take them to their hotel. It wasn't one of the newer modern international hotels they passed on their drive from the airport but instead a much smaller and far more luxurious one in what, Saul explained to her, had originally been a rich merchant's private town house.

The present owners had obviously attempted to retain the ambience of the original building, the foyer and very grand staircase being hung with heavy, dark oil paintings, portraits in the main of sober-faced men and dutifully posed women and children.

The foyer was illuminated by a huge chandelier, while the discreet uniforms of the hotel staff reflected the sombre but rich colours of the portraits.

Whether by accident or design, Tullah didn't know, but the foyer smelled deliciously of spices—cinnamon, nutmeg and others she couldn't recognise.

Sniffing the air appreciatively, she was unable to stop herself asking Saul eagerly, "Was the merchant who built this place connected with the Dutch East Indies?"

Her question drew an unexpectedly approving smile from Saul.

"Yes, as a matter of fact he was. Not many people are so quick to make the connection between the spices still used to scent the air and the trade that led to the house being built."

"It must have been wonderfully exciting waiting for a cargo to arrive from so far away."

"Mmm...providing it *did* arrive and the ship hadn't been boarded by pirates or, more mundanely, its cargo ruined by salt water, or the profits eaten up by the bribes the merchants had to pay." When he saw Tullah's crestfallen expression, Saul's smile broadened slightly as he agreed ruefully, "Very well, yes, it must have been exciting, exciting and romantic and almost beyond our modern comprehension to appreciate what it must have been like to complete such a journey from one side of the world to the other, relying on nothing but skill, hope and the wind and tide."

"The porter will show you to your rooms," the receptionist announced with a smile when she finished checking their booking forms. As they turned to go, she added to Saul, "I'm afraid the rooms we've allocated to you will not be quite so nice as the two-bedroomed suite that was first booked, but we hope you will have a comfortable stay with us."

As he turned to join her, Saul told Tullah quietly, "Marsha had originally booked a suite, two separate bedrooms linked by a shared sitting room so that Derek and I could spend some time going over everything and discussing another case we've got pending more easily than if we'd had separate rooms. However, I asked Marsha to change the booking this morning so that neither of us would feel compromised by being in a situation that others might misinterpret."

Tullah stared at him. Such forethought and consideration went totally against everything she believed about him and took her so off guard that she simply couldn't think of anything to say.

"It's going on for four now," Saul told her, flicking back his cuff to glance at his watch. "I suggest we give ourselves half an hour to unpack and then I'll take you down to the court where the case will be held so that you can familiarise yourself with everything. I've got a business meeting this evening but it won't be a late night, so please don't hesitate to give my room a ring if, during the course of the evening, you come across any potential problems with the case.

"It's going to be an early start in the morning. Hopefully, if your information is correct, things should be fairly cut and dried and then, of course, we're having dinner with Claus van der Laurens that evening. The lifts are this way...."

Silently Tullah followed him. She had no idea why she should suddenly feel so...so alone, just because he had told her that he was going out for dinner...*without* her.

CHAPTER EIGHT

TULLAH took a deep breath.

"And we give in evidence a copy of the patent, signed and dated in accordance with our claim, accompanied by a copy of the original letter confirming the sale and transfer of that patent from the original owner to the corporation, together with a copy of the deed of assignment."

On the other side of the courtroom, she could feel Saul watching her and automatically she found herself turning her head to meet his fixed, unwavering gaze. She hadn't wanted to look at him, to give him the impression that she felt in any way in need of his support or his approval, and yet whilst she waited for the evidence she had just submitted to be studied, she was intensely conscious of an almost magnetic bond between them, a sense of closeness…comradeship, of being united, which couldn't be analysed away by logic or argument.

Twenty-four hours ago she would have declared

quite vehemently that she had no need of Saul to share a victory and certainly no desire for him to witness a defeat, and yet as the tension within the courtroom grew, she was increasingly aware of the sense of strength and calm she was drawing from Saul's silent presence.

There was nothing quite like the atmosphere in a courtroom to make you feel vulnerable and isolated, Tullah reminded herself, and the intimacy it could create between members of the same legal team could make for very strange bedfellows in the real world beyond its four walls.

Bedfellows?

Her heart skipped a beat, and on the other side of the room as though he had registered it, felt it with her, she saw Saul's eyebrows draw together in a sharp frown.

Her evidence was still being considered. She tried not to betray any nervousness and to remain completely impassive. She was in no doubt whatsoever as to the validity of the corporation's claim, or the fact that the twenty-five-year patent did indeed take precedence over the other side's much shorter patent, but as Saul had warned her this morning, it never paid to be too confident, and for all they knew the other side could produce last-minute evidence of which they had no knowledge.

What if there was something she *had* missed in her research, some evidence she had overlooked? She could feel herself starting to panic a little. Bad enough to lose the case and with it one of the corporation's most valuable patents, but to lose it in front of Saul… Despite the silent visual bonding that existed between them now, once the case was over she knew that things would return to normal, that they would once again be antagonists, and that she must not read too much into the mental support she could almost feel him sending out to her.

The other side had been aggressive in their determination to win the case, but to her relief they had not produced any new evidence. Tullah could feel the tension cramping her stomach muscles, the only sound breaking the silence being the steady rustle of papers as the court studied both sets of evidence.

What was Saul thinking? Did *he* think they would win? Was there anything that *he* might have done to secure the verdict they needed that she had not?

It seemed a lifetime before the clerk to the court

finally announced that the court was ready to deliver its verdict.

Tullah held her breath as she stood up, her face professionally impassive, but she couldn't quite resist darting another quick look at Saul. Seeking what? Reassurance? Confirmation that he was pleased with the way she had handled the case? Neither was she able to resist the temptation to give in to the extremely unprofessional urge to cross her fingers and offer up a small prayer for success.

The verdict was read out slowly and carefully. Tullah took a deep breath of relief as she heard the confirmation of the validity and authenticity of the corporation's patent.

Suddenly she became aware of things she hadn't noticed before, like the fact that the sun was streaming in through the courtroom windows and that outside, away from the hushed, awesome atmosphere of the courtroom, normal, everyday life was still taking place. She could hear the sound of cars, people passing, someone whistling.

She took another deep breath and felt the relief flood through her like a burst of effervescent, giddiness-inducing bubbles of happiness.

"Well done!"

This time she didn't move away when she felt Saul's touch on her arm, instead simply standing where she was, too relieved to attempt to hide her feelings from him, her own hand going to her throat as she admitted huskily, "I was afraid that they might find against us, even though I knew our patent was valid. Silly of me, I know," she added ruefully.

"Not silly at all. On the contrary, an eminently sensible reaction, I would have said," Saul contradicted her, explaining when she looked questioningly at him, "Overconfidence can be as dangerous as ignorance. To be aware that there could be hazards, pitfalls, is to be ready to deal with them, as you did."

"I *did* have a couple of bad moments when the other side tried to claim that the original patent holder had had a change of heart and had written to the corporation informing them that he was only prepared to sell them the patent for a period of ten years." Tullah paused hesitantly. "Do you think—"

"No," Saul interjected crisply, shaking his head. "In my view that was simply a delaying tactic to hold things up in court…an attempt to get the court to make a ruling that more research was needed to check out the existence of such a document. Totally unprofitable from their point of view, but while such research was going on, all the income from the patent would have had to remain frozen, of course, which would have had a dire effect on our profits. Even an organisation the size of Aarlston isn't immune to a take-over bid, and if you want my opinion, I'm half-inclined to suspect that there could be something more behind this claim that the original patent was invalid."

"You mean some third party could have been behind it in an attempt to destabilize the corporation's financial position?"

"Well, it *has* been known," Saul told her dryly. "However, on this occasion at least, if there *was* something underhand going on behind the scenes..." He gave a small shrug. "You did very well, especially since you were rather thrown in at the deep end."

"I *was* very nervous," Tullah admitted. Suddenly it seemed the most natural thing in the world to admit to him how apprehensive she had felt. The relief, the euphoria, she was experiencing at winning the case had produced a sense of closeness, of comradeship with Saul that for the moment pushed aside all other considerations and differences. She was even rather glad of the protective arm he extended to her as he shielded her from the surge of people leaving the court, welcoming the courtliness of an old-fashioned male gesture of chivalry and ruefully admitting that her feminine instincts were overwhelming her more modern awareness of the rules of equality and political correctness.

"I'd suggest a celebration lunch," Saul offered, "but it's a bit on the late side now, and…"

Tullah shook her head. "I don't really feel like eating," she told him regretfully. "What I really need is to go up to my room and to write my report while everything is still fresh in my mind."

"Mmm…well, if you're sure you don't mind, there *is* something I'd rather wanted to do," Saul informed her without specifying what it was. "Claus is sending a car to collect us at seven-thirty, by the way."

"I'll be ready," Tullah assured him.

Now that the ordeal of the court hearing was successfully behind her, she was actually looking forward to meeting the founder of the corporation, even though Saul was going to be there, as well.

Even though…

She paused, unable to resist sneaking a quick look at him. Something rather odd was taking place within her, some extraordinary and unexpected cocktail of emotions and responses that were combining together to give her a feeling of light-heartedness and excitement…a sense of anticipation and actual physical breathlessness.

Someone pushed past them, forcing her to move closer to Saul. Immediately his hold on her tightened and he looked down at her—and kept on looking.

He really had the most exceptionally beautiful eyes, their colour so deep, so warm that… And as for his eyelashes… She lifted her hand, wanting to touch them to see if they felt as soft and silky as they looked, and then stopped, dizzily gulping in a lungful of air. What on earth was she thinking? Doing…?

"Tullah."

Saul was leaning closer to her, concern momentarily darkening his eyes, like shadows crossing the sun.

A heightened sensation of portent, of standing

on the edge of something vital and life changing shook her, a feeling of uncannily clear-minded perception that suddenly, here and now, in this mundane setting with people bustling to and fro around her, she was facing something immensely important.

Saul lifted his hand towards her face and already in her mind's eye she could see it cupping her jaw, feel its warmth…its power…its passion…its…*his* ability to change her whole life simply by the act of touching her; that once he *did* touch her, nothing could or would be the same again.

Like a sleepwalker, she gave a deep shudder and wrenched her glance away from his, stepping back from him, allowing the busy crowd to surge between them.

"I…I must go," she told him stiltedly. Then without giving him any chance to respond, she started to walk away, to walk and then to run, driven by a sense of panic that far outmatched the apprehension she had experienced before the trial. This was different; this was personal…this was…

Anxiously she remembered reading somewhere of an American experiment that had proved that a man was more likely to find a woman attractive, to fall in love with her, if he saw her immediately following some kind of adrenalin-raising experience or after an incident that either challenged or alarmed him, but surely the same thing did not apply to a woman. Surely *women* were immune from that sort of vulnerability.

And yet she couldn't possibly be attracted to Saul; there was just no way. Carefully she sifted through the evidence listing all the reasons why it was simply not possible, starting to breathe a sigh of relief as they mounted up, incontrovertible, solid and deeply rooted.

All that was on the other side of the scales, all that the prosecution case had to challenge her defence was a mere sensation, a ripple of feeling, a sense of something indefinable and electric, a feather in other words that could in no way hope to outbalance the heavy, solid weight it opposed.

Still, tormentingly, it remained there, so ephemeral that it could be blown away by the merest breath of reality and logic. But annoyingly, it refused to fade away, returning each time she attempted to banish it to lie tantalisingly there on the other side of the scales, refusing all her attempts to ignore it.

One look; one missed heartbeat; one brief sensation of dizzy breathlessness; one peculiar awareness of a portentous event taking place… What, after all, did they mean? What *were* they other than merely the product of an overworked imagination? They were nothing, the merest… the merest feather…nothing…nothing at all, and certainly not worth the bother of pursuing or worrying over.

She had other things to do. Other plans for the rest of the afternoon—like Saul. Saul. Here she was, coming full circle thinking about him yet again.

The Mauritshuis was virtually empty, allowing Tullah to enjoy the luxury of wandering slowly from painting to painting at her leisure, to absorb the full richness of the master's use of colour and form, light and shade, to enjoy the small details of each great work as she studied the Vermeer collection she had come to see.

A voluptuous sigh of pleasure passed her lips as she stood in front of one of her favourites, his *View of Delft*. Lost in her study of it, she wasn't aware of someone else approaching the painting until a brief movement caught her eye. Turning her head, she froze as she saw Saul watching her.

"What are you doing here?" she demanded.

"Much the same as you," he responded dryly. "You like Vermeer?" he asked her, nodding in the direction of the painting she was studying.

"Like?" Tullah's mouth curled in scornful contempt. "One doesn't merely *like* a work of this order," she told him pithily.

She stopped abruptly as she realised he was teasing her, laughter lines crinkling the corner of his eyes.

"You look like Meg when something's made her cross," he observed good-humouredly. "I hope you aren't going to stamp your feet."

Tullah shot him a venomous look. How on earth had she ever thought him attractive, ever worried that she might be in danger of finding or wanting…?

"If I ever stamp my feet, it will be because you're under them," she told him sweetly.

Saul's eyebrows rose. "I'm all for a woman being strong and being able to assert herself," Saul returned after a small pause, "but there does come a point when such assertiveness becomes almost an act of aggression, and you—"

"I what?" Tullah snapped, challenging him.

Saul shook his head. "Forget it," he said sardonically. "There's just no way to win with you, is there, Tullah? Take care, though, that you don't misjudge the enemy you're so determined to destroy. You might just find that you're the one you've impaled on your sharp little verbal thorns."

So saying, he turned on his heel and walked away from her, leaving Tullah to watch him go.

"Come on, you cannot leave me on my own to finish this bottle of wine, and I know there is no point in pressing Saul to take another glass for he is an abstemious man and can never be persuaded to act against his own judgement."

As Tullah half-heartedly tried to protest when Claus van der Laurens insisted on refilling her glass with the extremely rich and delicious red wine he had ordered with their meal as a celebration of Tullah's equally fine triumph in court earlier in the day, she was forced to acknowledge that the founder of the corporation quite obviously held Saul in very high esteem. And not just that, he actively liked Saul and treated him with an almost avuncular warmth.

And if such a patently shrewd and astute man as Claus van der Laurens thought so highly of Saul, then where did that leave her and her own negative and antagonistic feelings towards him?

From their conversation this evening, it was obvious that the Dutchman was a committed family man, who had explained to Tullah that the only reason his wife was not joining them was because their eldest granddaughter had just had a baby and she had gone to stay with her to help.

"Saul was telling me that you share our passion for one of our great painters," the older man commented as Tullah drank her wine.

"Yes. Yes, I do," she agreed, frowning a little. What else had Saul told Claus van der Laurens about her? Nothing, she hoped, that might prove detrimental to her career.

"I have a small interior after his style by one of his pupils," the older man was telling her, shaking his head as he went on to admit, "It is very good in its way, but once you have seen the work of the master..."

"It's his eye for detail," Tullah responded, but her mind wasn't really on her favourite painter.

It was impossible, of course, that she could be wrong in her assessment and judgement of Saul but… But there was no doubt that her view of him did seem to be in conflict with the high regard in which others quite obviously held him. Which meant what exactly? That they were wrong and she was right or…

There was no doubt that he *was* an extremely sexually charismatic man. She had only to watch the reaction of the other women in the restaurant to his presence to know that…or to acknowledge the physical reactions of her own body, she reminded herself ruefully.

Their host was now discussing the soon-to-be-held Masquerade Ball at which he and his family were to be honourary guests of the corporation.

It was well past midnight before they finally left the restaurant and Saul hailed a taxi to take them back to their hotel. There was something about sharing the dark interior of a taxi late at night with an extremely sexy and attractive man that was quite definitely unsettling, Tullah told herself, or at least that was her excuse for the dangerous and highly provocative awareness of Saul as a man that she seemed to be developing.

Determined to ignore such ridiculous and untenable feelings, she deliberately averted her head from him and stared out into the darkness beyond the cab window, but at one point when they were in a short queue of standing traffic, she suddenly felt compelled to turn her head and look at him.

To her shock, Saul was looking back at her, his eyes narrowing briefly as they studied one another in silence. Tullah was the first to look away but not before her glance had dropped betrayingly to his mouth.

It must be the wine that was affecting her, she decided as the taxi came to a halt outside the hotel. It had been extremely vigorous and full-bodied and, she suspected, far stronger than she had originally suspected. She didn't feel drunk, or indeed anything like it, she just felt…she just felt… She just felt intrigued to know what it would be like to be kissed by Saul, whether it was true what they said about men with that particular type of sensually curved bottom lip. Would he be the type to rush and spoil things, greedily grasping at more intimate pleasures or would he take his time, sensuously exploring and enjoying to the full the delicious intimacy of a long, lingering and very passionate kiss.

Would he…?

"I think it might be as well if you booked an early-morning call, given the fact that our flight leaves at ten," Saul warned her dryly, cutting across the highly volatile nature of her unfamiliarly erotic thoughts.

"What are you trying to say?" Tullah demanded, drawing herself up to her full height and taking a deep breath, the effect of which on the full curves of her body causing a man standing several yards away to stare open-mouthed in awe at her and wish enviously that he was in Saul's shoes. In these days of bone-thin women, it was a rare treat to see a woman shaped as a woman should be, all delectable, delicious feminine curves.

Tullah, who saw the hard look Saul was giving him but had no idea what was the cause of it, wondered what on earth he had done to cause Saul to look at him with such hostility before telling Saul imperiously, "As a matter of fact, I have already booked a call, but if by that remark you were trying to imply that I've…that I'm…"

She started to founder slightly in the face of Saul's lack of encouragement and the cool, raised-eyebrowed look he was giving her.

"I'm not drunk," she told him, spoiling for a fight, then gave a small, betraying hiccup. "I only had four glasses," she started to protest as Saul led the way towards the bank of lifts.

"Four glasses but virtually a whole bottle," Saul murmured dryly.

Tullah gasped and attempted to deny it, offering plaintively, "Claus kept refilling my glass…."

"Exactly," Saul agreed sardonically, warning her, "I just hope you've got some headache remedy with you because I suspect you're going to need it in the morning."

"Really, Saul, you're such a killjoy," Tullah snapped.

"It's not a matter of being a killjoy," Saul returned calmly. "More a case of knowing Claus. He's a generous host, but he's got a head like cast iron. I've seen him drink his way through a couple of bottles of vintage wine and not show the slightest effect, but it can have a pretty lethal kickback if you're not used to drinking it."

Tullah opened her mouth to point out that she was a woman nearing thirty and that she was perfectly capable of knowing when she had had too much to drink, but just at that moment the lift arrived, disgorging its passengers, and the moment was lost.

As it was, she had no illusions about the reason why Saul was so insistent on walking her to her bedroom door, and it had nothing to do with any desire on his part to inveigle his way into her room or her bed.

"I'm perfectly sober," she informed him crossly as he removed the passcard from her hand and slid it into the lock.

"Now what are you doing?" she demanded when he pushed open the door for her and then followed her into her room. "I'm not one of your children, you know. You don't have to stand over me while I get undressed or to make sure I've cleaned my teeth properly before I go to bed…."

She frowned as he ignored her and disappeared in the direction of the bathroom, reappearing with a glass, then opening the minibar to extract a bottle of water, which he uncapped and poured into the glass.

"Drink this," he told her tersely. "It probably won't do anything to avert the inevitable hangover you're going to have in the morning but it might at least go some way to stop you being totally dehydrated."

"Yes, *Daddy*," Tullah mocked pseudo meekly, taking the glass from him. But somehow she managed to let it slip from her grasp and the shock of the ice-cold water soaking through her top and on to her skin made her gasp in outraged shock.

"Now look what you've done," she accused Saul as she started to tug the wet fabric away from her body.

She thought she heard Saul curse under his breath as he disappeared into the bathroom for a second time but she was too involved in trying to remove her damp clothes, peeling off first her top and then her silky bra and dropping them on the floor with a brief moan of distaste.

"Here, take this..." she heard Saul instructing her grimly, but when she turned round, looking at him unsteadily, surprised to realise that he was still in her room, she saw the look of shock register in his eyes, his jaw becoming rigid as he grated, "Just what the hell do you think you're doing?"

What was she doing?

Tullah gave him a puzzled look. What did he mean? She wasn't *doing* anything. She was just... As she looked from his angry, disbelieving face to the clothes she had discarded, enlightenment suddenly dawned. She gave a small giggle and then another and then teased him coquettishly, "What's wrong, Saul? Haven't you ever seen a woman without her clothes on before?"

She gave him a mock demure pout and thought

she heard him say devoutly, "Oh my God, I just don't believe this! Claus, you've got a hell of a lot to answer for." Whilst the giggles still bubbled up inside her like young champagne, Saul thrust the towel he was carrying towards her and told her grittily, "Here, cover yourself up with this."

"I don't want to be covered up," Tullah countered, pouting naughtily. "What's wrong, Saul?" she cooed. "Don't you like my body? Most men…"

"Good Lord, I've had enough of this. Stand still," Saul ordered angrily as he attempted to wrap the towel around her.

Tullah laughed. "It won't stay up like that," she warned him. "You'll have to wrap it tight and tuck the end in here." Roguishly she touched the vee of flesh between her breasts and then taunted saucily, "What is it, Saul? Don't you *want* to touch me?"

"What I want right now," Saul snapped, his temper frayed beyond repair, "is to go to bed."

"And what?" Tullah breathed, taking a step closer to him. For some reason she didn't seem able to remove her gaze from his mouth and stared at it in open curiosity and fascination.

"Tullah," Saul warned.

He knew she had no real idea of what she was doing; that it was the expensive mature wine she had drunk that was the primary cause of her sudden lack of inhibitions rather than any personal feelings for him. But my God, didn't she have *any* idea just *what* she was doing to him, just *what* the sight of those magnificent naked breasts were doing to him and what he wanted to do to them, with them, to her? He'd have to be made of stone to resist the tantalising message of innocence and allure she was sending out, never mind feeling about her the way…

"Tullah…" he groaned, and this time there was a tiny flicker of nervous recognition in the look she gave him but it was too little, too late, and he dropped the towel he had been holding and scooped her up in his arms.

"Saul…" Tullah breathed ecstatically, her eyes widening with surprised pleasure. "Kiss me," she begged him impetuously. "I want you to kiss me now." And just to emphasise her point, she leaned forward in his arms, wrapping her own tightly round him as she pressed her mouth on his.

Men who took advantage of too tipsy women were in Saul's opinion beneath contempt, beyond the pale, and he was quite definitely not and had never wanted to be counted amongst their company.

It was a man's responsibility to be protective of a woman, to safeguard her even when she herself… He, after all, had daughters of his own, young girls who would one day be in much the same vulnerable position as Tullah was now. Just what would he think of some male, *any* male, who dared to take advantage of their innocence… their…?

"Saul," Tullah murmured provocatively into his mouth.

It was no good, it was too late, and it was impossible to resist the invitation she was so artlessly and irresistibly offering him. Didn't she *know* how much he…but how could she when…?

Saul closed his eyes and succumbed to the temptation to enjoy the soft, delicate movement of her mouth against his as she tried to tease and coax a response from him.

Tullah gave a small quivering breath of disappointment. Saul wasn't going to respond to her, he wasn't going to kiss her and now she would never know. She was just about to lift her mouth from his when totally unexpectedly his mouth hardened on hers, taking control of the kiss, taking control of *her* as he expertly turned the tables on her and started to move his mouth caressingly against hers. A tiny quiver of sensation ran through her and then another. She tried to breathe and found she couldn't and then she tried to pull away from him and found she couldn't do that, either. And what was worse, she didn't really want to.

For a moment, she tried to resist and then dizzily gave in to the dangerous thrill of excitement that was making her tremble from head to foot as she responded eagerly to his kiss.

She could never remember being kissed by anyone like this before…or kissing anyone like this before. No, certainly not that. In fact, she could hardly recognise herself in this sensual, uninhibited woman who was not merely responding but actively inciting and prolonging the delicious sensations of the slow, lingering kisses that were gradually becoming more and more intimate and passionate.

Was it really her making those sexy little noises of pleasure and approval that were causing Saul to hold her even tighter and explore the soft secrets of her mouth even more lingeringly?

Her heart was beating so fast it felt as though it was going to burst through the wall of her chest.

She was sure that Saul must be able to feel it. How could he not do when he was holding her so close, when…?

He was kissing her more slowly now, more deeply. Mmm… Tullah gave a soft, slow sigh of sensual pleasure, opening her eyes to look up into Saul's and then going breathless and dizzy when she saw the way he was looking back at her, recognising the extent of his arousal from the dilation of his pupils. Bemused, she reached out and touched his face with her hand, awed as much by his reaction to her as she was by her own to him.

Knowing that he was aroused and vulnerable created a bond between them, a shared if unvocalised awareness of their mutual inexplicable and irrational reaction to one another, their shared desire and need. In her heightened emotional state of mind and with her inhibitions and normal controls so relaxed she couldn't help but respond to this attraction and to him.

There was a wonderful, exhilarating sense of release and freedom in being able to express her emotional and physical needs so openly and easily, in being able to cast aside her guard and acknowledge, admit, that the desire for him, which she was now allowing to express itself, had been there virtually from the first time they met. It existed even if she herself had tried to force it underground and keep it hidden away, denying it out of her fear of repeating the pattern of both her childhood and her teenage years when she had loved men who were both unworthy of her love and incapable of returning it.

But Saul wasn't like that. This time it would be different, this time…

She gave a small, blissful sigh as she snuggled closer to him, pressing her body lovingly against his. "Saul," she breathed, her imagination teasing her senses with vividly sensual promises. "Let's go to bed…I want you to take me to bed…."

The groan Saul gave wasn't caused entirely by the knowledge that she was quite obviously still a long, long way from sobering up. The feel of her body against his, the innocently sensuous way she was moving against him, were taxing his self-control to its limits, beyond its limits, he ruefully admitted as he fought and lost the battle to control his own response to her.

And she knew what was happening to him, of course. He could see it in the half-veiled, femininely triumphant look she gave him as she let her glance travel very slowly and deliberately down his body before looking back into his eyes.

"Saul," she whispered throatily.

Perhaps if she hadn't already been half-naked, perhaps if he hadn't given in to the temptation to hold her and to kiss her, it might have been different, but he *had* done so, and having done so, he made one last desperate attempt to avert the inevitable by telling her gruffly, "Tullah, I can't..."

The pouting but very pointed look she gave his lower body accompanied by the claim "Liar' told him that she had misunderstood.

Holding her gently, he tried to explain. "No. I mean we can't...I don't have any...I can't..."

Enlightenment dawned in Tullah's eyes.

"Oh, that's all right," she told him happily. "I do. They're in the bathroom." She paused when she saw the rather shocked look he wasn't able to control.

Perhaps he was being old-fashioned, but Tullah had never struck him as the kind of woman who went in for casual sex, very much the opposite in fact. Despite her professional qualifications and ability, there was a gentleness and hesitancy about her that had led him to believe that her sexual experience was limited, her lovers few rather than many, but now it seemed…

"Weren't there any in yours?" she asked him, frowning slightly. "I thought it must be something the hotel did automatically, this being Holland and…"

Saul started to smile. "I don't know," he replied. "There may well have been. I didn't notice."

"So you see, we *can* after all," she murmured as she reached up to touch him. "Mmm…that feels good," she told him huskily as he gave in to the temptation to caress the full, warm curve of her breast.

"Not half as good as it's going to feel," Saul assured her thickly as he swung her up into his arms and then gently lowered her on to the bed as Tullah clasped her hands behind his head and lifted her face towards his for his kiss.

Mmm…kissing was a highly underrated activity and one that was a vastly unexplored territory in her CV of life experiences, Tullah decided dazedly as she wrapped her arms even more firmly around Saul and held him closer.

She could feel his hands caressing her body, stroking gently over her skin, and it felt wonderful. She drew a long, ecstatic breath of feminine pleasure, arching her spine in voluptuous encouragement at the same time reaching out to tug impatiently at the shirt he was wearing, protesting beneath his kisses, "It's not fair. You can touch me, but I can't touch you…."

"Do you want to touch me?" Saul responded.

Dreamily Tullah looked into his eyes and then let her glance slide appreciatively over his body, feeling the sudden acceleration of female excitement at the potency of her secret and hitherto forbidden thoughts and desires.

"Yes," she told him boldly. "Yes, I do."

For a moment, the sudden fierce pleasure of male passion in his eyes made her falter and feel a little self-conscious and nervous. Then Saul was releasing her and easing himself a little way back from her. He rapidly unfastened his shirt and shrugged it off before inviting her thickly, "Come on then, go ahead."

She hesitated. Somehow the close physical proximity of a man, a real man whose torso was slightly roughened by thick, silky dark hair and whose skin gleamed with a faint sheen that had nothing to do with some expensive grooming aid and everything to do with the way he was reacting to her as a man, was having such an overwhelming aphrodisiacal effect on her senses that she actually felt faint with the intensity of her own desire. She found herself unable to make up her mind what she wanted to do the most. Perhaps simply look at him, reach out and touch him exploratively with her fingertips or—her heart lurched crazily against her chest—give in to the shockingly unfamiliar grown-up, womanly adult need to lean forward and place her lips against his skin to breathe in the scent of him, to touch him, kiss him, taste him, feel every life breath he took, and with it feel, too, his male reaction to her.

"If you keep looking at me like that we're going to experience the safest sex it's possible for two people to have," Saul warned her grittily, adding rawly, "at least for the first time. It's been a long time for me, Tullah, and my body's reacting to you more like a teenage boy's than an adult male's. I can't—"

"How long?" Tullah asked him curiously.

He paused before answering her, his mouth compressing before he told her curtly, "Hillary and I have been separated for over two years and before that… If you want the honest answer, it must be all of two or three—"

"Months," Tullah supplied.

Saul was frowning. "Two or three months? Try again. You've got the numbers right but the period of time wrong. Two or three *years* was what I was about to say," he told her flatly. "And if you want the real truth, the last time was actually before Meg's birth and even before that..."

Tullah stared at him.

That couldn't be true, surely, but Saul didn't look or sound as though he was lying to her. Maybe the intoxicating wine she had drunk was still clouding her thoughts. She looked up into his eyes and asked him teasingly, "If I help you with the rest of your clothes, will you help me with mine?"

It was more than Saul could resist. *She* was more than he was able to resist. A direct approach for sex even from a woman he wanted as much as he wanted Tullah he might have been able to resist, but when it was coupled with her sense of humour, her warmth, her sheer lovability and his own feelings for her, it was just too much for his self-control. *She* was just too much for his self-control.

He took hold of her hand and started to kiss the tip of each finger and then slowly and lingeringly suck on them, drawing them into his mouth until Tullah felt she would either faint or burst with the pleasure he was giving her.

Later she couldn't remember how or when they finally got undressed, whether it was before he started to stroke the palm of her hand and then the inside of her wrist with the tip of his tongue or after he had started to draw the same tantalising nerve-shattering circles of scarcely bearable sensual pleasure around the ripe crests of her breasts, finally drawing each nipple into his mouth and caressing it until she moaned out loud in pleasure and need.

All she *did* know was that at some point she was deliciously, wondrously free to touch and caress him, all of him, everywhere and anywhere she liked, to pleasure him and to pleasure herself with her wide-eyed exploration of his flesh and her uninhibited appreciation of his maleness and his response to her. And when she poutingly refused to allow him to leave her in order to take advantage of the hotel's provisions for safe sex, he told her softly that there were other ways he could pleasure her, pleasure them *both*, and she was too caught up in the emotional and sexual intensity of the moment to either object or to protest that it was not an intimacy she was used to, that it was not an intimacy she had shared with anyone else.

Which surely must have been why, when he laid her gently on the bed and slowly parted her thighs, she made no objection, watching him dreamily as he caressed her tenderly with his fingers before his passion finally overwhelmed him and he bent his head and placed his mouth on her, possessing her with a hot, eager hunger that made her heart race and her body burn, the fierce flood of desire that seized her catching her so off guard that she cried out in shock against it. But it was too late. The strong spiral of climactic urgency had already begun and there was no turning back, no stopping what Saul's passionate intimacy had started.

And no stopping, either, the languorous tide of exhaustion that inevitably swept over her. As she lay at peace in Saul's arms, he smiled wryly as he watched her eyes close and felt sleep slacken her body.

It would be cruel to wake her up, even if his body ached for her so badly that…that staying here in bed was not a good idea, he warned himself firmly. The *last* thing he wanted to do was to prejudice their newly burgeoning relationship by coming across as the kind of man who selfishly demanded satisfaction of his own desire.

Reluctantly he edged his body away from her, pausing only to kiss her briefly on the tip of her nose before pulling on his clothes and quietly leaving.

CHAPTER NINE

TULLAH awoke with the alarm call, the shrill noise jolting her awake and drawing an agonized gasp of pain as she opened her eyes and recognised that she was suffering from one of her thankfully rare migraine headaches no doubt brought on, as she brutally reminded herself, not just by the stress of her court appearance but by her overindulgence in last night's red wine.

Of course, she hadn't brought any painkillers with her...of course, and she doubted that there would be time to get any on their way to the airport. She still had to shower and dress and pack, but mercifully she wasn't expected to put in an appearance at breakfast. The last person she wanted to see right now was Saul Crighton, and not just because she felt so thoroughly under the weather and because she could remember his frowning firm refusal of more than one glass of wine last night.

She might only have a very hazy recollection of

events once Saul had ushered her into the taxi, but she had the most extraordinary and blush-making clear memories of the vividly erotic dreams she had had last night and the man who had partnered her in them...*partnered* her! The way *she* had dreamt it, *she* had been the one doing most of the chasing. Mercifully, though, no one other than her was ever likely to know about that or about the way things had felt...the sheer sensuality of the desire she had experienced...shared...shown, least of all Saul.

There was a perfectly rational explanation of why she should have dreamt about Saul Crighton with such sexual explicitness, she decided hastily, and perhaps once her migraine had gone she would be able to find it.

It was humiliating, though, to be forced to confront the fact that the secret she had believed she had so safely hidden away, even from herself, had not been as well hidden as she had thought after all.

Of course, it was inappropriate and illogical that she should be so aware of Saul as a man, but all she had to keep doing to suppress those feelings...those emotions, was to remind herself of what he really was and that was most certainly not the tender, passionate, sensual lover who had shared her dream, but rather a weak parody of all that she believed a man should really be. Yes, he had the looks, the air, the outer garb of real masculinity, but they were simply a mask and meant nothing…just as last night's dream meant nothing.

Ouch… She winced as she slid out of bed and her head started to pound sickeningly. She really shouldn't have drunk all that wine.

"Are you sure you're all right?"

No, of course she wasn't all right, far from it, but Saul was the last person she was going to admit as much to, Tullah acknowledged as she turned towards him and snapped, "Yes. I'm fine… it's just a headache, that's all."

They had boarded the plane ten minutes earlier and the act of taking off had left Tullah gritting her teeth and feeling as though her head was about to explode.

Just one word, just one sentence, from Saul that included the words "hangover' or "wine' and she would thump him, Tullah promised herself bitterly as she closed her eyes and prayed for the pounding inside her skull to ease.

Saul, as expected, had no such problem, his head bent over the newspaper he was reading.

Tullah could hear the flight attendants coming round with trays of food, but the mere thought of eating made her feel acutely nauseous and she knew if her migraine took its normal and thankfully rare course, that it would be at least a day, possibly two, before she was anything like back to normal.

The migraine attacks had first started when her parents were divorcing and had grown in intensity during her teenage years to the point where she was having one virtually every few weeks. In her twenties, though, they had become less and less frequent and it was now over a year since she had suffered her last one.

This one, though, promised to be a real horror, but right now the reason she was beginning to wince wasn't so much the vivid flashes of light that burned across her closed eyes but the even more vivid flashes of scenes from last night's dream that seared across her memory.

She couldn't help it. She gave a small, audible groan as one particular dream sequence presented itself to her. How could she have possibly dreamt herself saying that…doing that? She gave another protesting groan, reflecting feelingly that it was just as well that the human race was, for the most part, denied the ability to read one another's minds. She would *die*, just *die* if Saul Crighton should ever come *close* to guessing about the way she had dreamt of him, whispering to him that she wanted him to take his clothes off, that she wanted him to… And the worst thing of all was that her body, below migraine-feeling level, was totally oblivious to her mind's outraged primness and rejection of her dream and actually dared to respond to the implausible scenes it seemed she had created in her sleep, which meant… which meant that a part of her must actually have *wanted*…must actually have liked—

"Try to drink some water."

Tullah opened her eyes and grimaced, quickly closing them again to block out the sight of Saul's lean, tanned hand holding out a glass of water to her.

"Drink it," Saul insisted in much the same firm, authoritative voice Tullah had heard him use to his children. For a handful of seconds she toyed with mental relish the idea of refusing, but just as she was about to give in, Saul added grittily,

"I warned you last night that you'd be dehydrated after all that alcohol."

"I had three, four glasses of wine…four at the most," Tullah protested, "and I know what you're thinking and you're wrong. I haven't got a hangover. It's a migraine."

"We've already had this conversation," Saul reminded her.

Had they? Tullah couldn't remember having done so. In fact, she was guiltily aware that she couldn't recall very much at all after getting into the taxi with Saul, which was extremely irritating, given the unwanted clarity with which she kept on remembering last night's dream. Perhaps she had chosen the wrong career, she told herself. After last night she surely qualified for the job of writing the screenplay for Hollywood's hottest sex films.

"We'll be landing soon," Saul warned her.

When Tullah had arrived downstairs in the lobby this morning, ashen-faced and plainly in a very uncommunicative mood, he had thought at first it was simply because she was having second thoughts about last night, something he had already spent half the night warning himself to expect and the other trying to figure out a way of dealing with her expected rejection both of him and what they had shared. What he had not been prepared for—what he had never even begun to imagine might happen—was that she would act as though the events of the previous evening had simply never taken place and it had taken him a while to begin to understand why.

She wasn't *deliberately* ignoring the intimacy they had shared because she regretted it; she quite plainly and simply could not remember it, which was hardly flattering especially when he…

But what concerned him much more than his own ego right now was the fact that she was quite patently not at all well.

"It's a migraine," she had told him defensively and he had no reason to disbelieve her. For one thing, strong though last night's vintage wine had been, it certainly hadn't been potent enough to cause her to be as ill as she obviously was now.

As the plane started to make its descent, he shot a quick look at her. Her complexion looked waxily pale, her top lip ominously beaded with sweat, and he had noticed earlier the way she had reacted to the brightening of the plane cabin's lights, almost wincing as she closed her eyes against them. By the time the plane was taxiing down the runway, she was both shivering and perspiring.

"It's a migraine," she whispered protestingly, "a migraine. I'm not—"

"Yes. It's all right, I know," Saul assured her as he discreetly summoned the attendant and asked her if they could disembark ahead of the other passengers.

Whether because of their descent or not, Tullah didn't know, but for some reason the pounding pain inside her head and the bright flashing darts of light that accompanied it had intensified to such a pitch that she could barely breathe, never mind move. One side of her body felt oddly heavy and inert, and frighteningly when she tried to lift her arm, for some reason it just didn't seem to respond to the commands of her brain.

"Classic migraine symptoms," she thought she heard the attendant saying sympathetically to Saul as they both gently helped her to her feet. "I should know. I get them myself...."

Tullah tried to protest that she was fine, that she could manage, that there was no need for Saul to pick her up and carry her as though she was a baby, but the words simply wouldn't come.

She had a disjointed impression of movement

and pain, of warmth and cold, of the comforting, familiar smell of Saul and the far less pleasant smell of jet fuel and dirt, and then somehow or other they were inside a car and Saul was saying something to the driver.

Then came the drive, bumpy and unbearably uncomfortable, its blissful cessation and the even more blissful awareness of warmth and comfort, of anxious, childish voices, then the wonderful, wonderful peace and darkness of a welcoming bedroom.

She woke up once briefly and was groggily aware of someone helping her to undress, giving her a drink and some medication before firmly tucking her up in bed again and telling her to go back to sleep.

She could feel the medication starting to do its work slowly, oh, so slowly; the tentacles of pain were beginning to unwrap themselves from inside her head.

"What's wrong with Tullah, Daddy?" Meg asked her father as she stood anxiously on one leg just inside the open bedroom door.

For the past four hours all of them had been under strict instructions not to make any noise or go into Tullah's room. It had frightened Meg a bit when her daddy had come home carrying Tullah in his arms, but he had told them that she was going to be all right and that she had a very nasty headache.

Dr Julie had come and she and Daddy had had a long talk before Dr Julie had written something down, which she had given him, and then Daddy had put them all in the car and they had driven into town so that he could go to the chemist and get some special medicine for Tullah. Aunt Jenny had been in the chemist's, as well. She had told Daddy that Louise was home.

It had terrified the life out of him when Tullah had virtually collapsed on him as they were about to leave the aircraft. All he could think of all the way home was the dreadful stories one read in the press of people who had lost their lives through contracting one of the virulent forms of meningitis, so the first thing he had done after he had got Tullah home was to check to see if she was showing any signs of the warning rash and *not*, he was half-ashamed to admit, primarily out of fear for his children.

No. His *primary* fear had been for her, for Tullah

herself, for the woman who had somehow or other got past the barriers he had in self-preservation erected against her sex. The woman who—

"When is she going to wake up?" Meg asked him.

"Not for a long time yet," he told her firmly, guessing what was coming next as he got up off the bed where he had been sitting and simply watching Tullah as she slept.

How was it possible for him to have fallen deeply in love so quickly and so completely when he had sworn that falling in love was something he was never going to allow himself to do? His life was, after all, complicated enough and he had already committed the sin of marrying their mother more out of lust and the mistaken belief that their mutual desire was a strong enough basis for marriage. He owed it to his children to put them first and to keep their lives free of any further emotional trauma. He hadn't wanted to love Tullah…he hadn't wanted to love *anyone*. There had, of course, been a time when he had thought…hoped…if he was honest, that he and Olivia…but that had been nothing more than a foolish clinging to a youthful infatuation and he had quickly recognised that Olivia had been right not to allow him to resurrect the past.

But what he felt for Tullah was different…different from anything he had ever felt before and he was amazed that he could ever have thought it possible to share his life with someone who was not Tullah, for whom he did not feel what he felt for Tullah.

But what, if anything, did she feel for him? She had wanted him last night…or had she? He knew a little of her past history from Olivia. There had been a man who had hurt her, a man quite patently nowhere near worthy of her, a man who, thankfully, had let her slip through his fingers.

It was gone four o'clock and he needed to go into the office. He leaned forward and kissed Tullah gently, smiling to himself as she continued to sleep.

"No, you aren't to wake her up," he reminded Meg sternly as he walked towards her.

"Where are you going?" Louise asked her mother. She had arrived home the previous day, irritated to discover that Saul was away on business and that she would have to wait until today to go and see him.

She knew full well that her parents did not approve of her love for Saul, but that was just too bad. She loved him and she was determined to have him.

"I'm going over to Saul's for him while he goes into work," Jenny informed her daughter. "He wants me to keep an eye on Tullah and the children."

"Tullah." Louise stiffened. She had heard Olivia talking about Tullah, an old friend of hers who had moved north to work for Aarlston's and who, she had been disconcerted to learn, had actually accompanied Saul to The Hague on business.

She had comforted herself with the knowledge that Saul was scarcely likely to be interested in her. His sole concern was for his children at the moment, but Louise was determined to change all that.

"What's she doing at Saul's?" she demanded suspiciously.

"Apparently she was ill on the journey home…a migraine. Saul took her home with him." Jenny paused as the phone started to ring. She picked up the receiver and immediately recognised the voice of the woman in charge of the private mother-and-baby home that Ruth and she had set up for young, single, local mothers and sighed, guessing that the call was likely to be a long one.

"Say," Louise hissed, "don't worry about Saul. I'll go over and stay with the kids."

"Louise," Jenny protested, but it was already too late. Louise had picked up Jenny's car keys and was opening the kitchen door.

Jenny sighed in exasperation, torn between responding to the urgency she could hear in her caller's voice and running after Louise to stop her going to Saul's, but in the end her sense of responsibility towards her commitment to her involvement in the single mothers' home had to take precedence, and as she held the receiver close to her ear, she watched Louise drive off in her car.

The single mothers' home had originally been Ruth's idea, born of her own secret pregnancy as a young woman when she had been forced to give up her child for adoption.

The wealth she had earned for herself in later years through her shrewd speculation on the stock market had enabled Ruth to buy the first special house she had formed as a short-stay hostel for young, unmarried mothers-to-be in need of somewhere to stay.

Now they were a registered charity with not

one house but closer on a dozen, plus a large, previously derelict mansion they had persuaded the local council to sell them at a knock-down price. Their charity had a royal patron and was funded, in the main, not only from local donations and the proceeds of the winter ball they held at Queensmead every year and a whole host of smaller social events, but also from street collections and a generous helping hand from Ruth herself.

Jenny had willingly become involved, working alongside Ruth in her venture, and was now a co-administrator of the charity. It was just as well that Guy Cooke, her partner in the local antiques shop they ran together, had been willing to give additional time to that business now that she was becoming more and more involved in the day-to-day administration of the charity and she could see the time coming when Guy would want to buy her out altogether.

However, as she listened to her caller, she was guiltily aware that her mind was not completely focused on the problem the woman was describing. The last thing Saul needed or wanted right now was to have Louise arriving on his doorstep. Her daughter's behaviour worried Jenny.

That she should have a crush on Saul wasn't particularly surprising given the fact that he was an extraordinarily good-looking man with just enough of a hint of tragedy in his circumstances and just enough maturity under his belt to appeal to a young and potentially very passionate girl on the verge of womanhood, but what *did* disturb Jenny was that Louise should be capable of pursuing Saul with such single-minded determination. It was so alien to her own experience. *She* had been a shy, rather awkward teenager who would never have dreamt of pursuing a man in the way that Louise was pursuing Saul. There were times when her daughter reminded her uncomfortably of her elder brother Max in her determined efforts to get what she wanted.

Both of them, it seemed, had inherited the selfish gene that had so clearly marked their uncle David, her husband's twin brother, and that thankfully was so completely lacking in Jon's much, much gentler make-up.

It was the commotion that woke Tullah—the sound of a child crying and the much sharper and far more angry sound of an older female voice telling her to stop.

"But you mustn't go in there. Daddy said we weren't to."

Tullah blinked as someone pushed open her bedroom door and the light flooded in. Blessedly, her migraine was gone but she still didn't feel entirely normal. The drugs didn't help, of course. These attacks always left her feeling enervated and weak, her brain somehow slightly numb.

She struggled to sit up as she vaguely recognised the tall, very angry-looking young woman who was standing in the doorway glowering at her and then made a grab for the duvet as she realised that someone had removed her clothes and that she was naked.

"Daddy undressed you," Meg informed her chattily. "He had to because you kept saying you were too hot."

Tullah gave the little girl a weak smile. "Meg," she exclaimed, turning to look uncertainly at her companion.

"This is Louise," Meg told her helpfully.

Louise…yes, of course. Well, Tullah could see why Saul would be interested in her. She was an extremely striking-looking girl although not exactly the timid, shy and rather naïve one Tullah had mentally visualised.

"Hello, I'm—"

But before Tullah could introduce herself properly, Louise was interrupting her to say tersely, "I know exactly who you are *and* what you're up to, but you're wasting your time. Saul is mine… and he's going to stay mine," she told Tullah challengingly.

Saul saw Jenny's car and then heard the commotion when he went from his study where he had been putting his papers together and walked into the bedroom. He discovered Louise standing at the foot of the bed, glowering ferociously at Tullah who was clutching the duvet around her body whilst Meg had crept on to the bed next to her and was huddled up beside her.

Swiftly assessing the situation, Saul reacted immediately, ignoring Louise to stride past her and take hold of Tullah's hand in both his own. As he sat next to her, he leaned forward to kiss the startled "Oh' that shaped her mouth.

"Good, you're awake. How are you feeling now, my darling?"

His darling…

Three pairs of female eyes focused on him.

In Louise's he could see furious disbelief and

in Tullah's he could see plain disbelief, but in Meg's… It seemed that Tullah had stolen more than one heart from this particular branch of the Crighton family, he acknowledged.

"You've arrived just in time to hear our good news, Louise," he continued, strategically angling his body so that Louise couldn't see Tullah's expression.

"What good news?" she demanded ominously.

"Tullah and I… Tullah and I are in love," he told her gently.

Behind him, he could hear Tullah gasp. In front of him, Louise's face went from white to red to white again.

"You can't possibly love her…you can't," she told Saul furiously. "I love you. I want you—and she won't stop me!" Then she turned on her heel and ran downstairs and out of the house.

Tullah winced as she heard the sound of the front door slamming.

"Why is Louise so angry?" Meg asked in a wavery voice.

Saul got up to follow her, turning to tell Tullah, "She's in no fit state to drive. I'll have to take her home and forget about going briefly into work."

He smiled at Meg who was watching him a little anxiously. "You look after Tullah for me until I get back, will you, Meggie? And make sure she doesn't get up."

Make sure she didn't get up. How *could* she, Tullah fumed after he had gone, when she had no idea where her clothes were…and just what had he meant by that comment to Louise that they were in love?

How could he have been so cruel to her when it was obvious how she felt about him?

She was still fuming half an hour later when he came back, gently telling Meg to go downstairs because he wanted to talk to Tullah on her own.

He wanted to talk to *her*!

"Would you mind telling me what all that was about or can I guess?" she demanded with heavy sarcasm.

"Yes. I know I owe you an explanation. The thing is…well, it's all a bit embarrassing, really. You see Louise believes…she thinks—"

"She's in love with you," Tullah finished bitingly.

"She's in love with the idea of being in love with

me," Saul corrected her mildly. "It's just a phase she's going through and I've—"

"You've what? You've got tired of basking in her innocent admiration, of playing with her emotions, and so you decided to use *me* as a means of getting rid of her. Well, for your information..."

She paused for breath and then frowned as she saw his expression. He interrupted her curtly. "You really think that...that I'd deliberately encourage a girl of that age to think...that my ego is such that...that I'm so vain and weak that I need that kind of adolescent...?" Saul stopped speaking to shake his head. "*Is* that what you really think?"

"Can you give me one good reason why I shouldn't?" Tullah asked him, but somehow instead of sounding challenging, her voice sounded rather more weak and defensive.

"I can give you any number," Saul informed her quietly, "not the least being the fact that she's a member of my family, young and vulnerable and... My God, she might be young enough to be my daughter," he told Tullah fiercely as he started to pace the floor. "Do you honestly believe—"

"It doesn't matter what *I* believe," Tullah interrupted him.

His reaction had shocked her. She had not expected him to react so vehemently or so intensely. His protest, his denials, seemed so genuine, but of course they couldn't be…could they?

"Your relationship with Louise is no concern of mine," she added forcefully as she tried to cling to the security of knowing that no matter how sexually attractive, no matter how emotionally attractive Saul might appear to be, he was, in fact, anything but.

But she might as well have tried to stop herself from sliding down a snow-covered hill, she acknowledged and was then unable to prevent herself from adding the pithy mental reminder that sliding down it accidentally was one thing, but wilfully throwing herself down it with total disregard for her safety was quite another.

"I don't *have* a relationship with Louise. At least not the type that *you're* trying to imply," Saul responded sharply.

"Well, you certainly could have fooled me," Tullah retorted. "Just like you tried to fool Louise that you and I… You'll have to tell her the truth. I don't want—"

"I *will* tell her the truth," Saul interjected, "but…"

"But what?" Tullah demanded suspiciously.

"But not yet." Whilst Tullah stared open-mouthed at him, he added, "You've seen for yourself, said yourself, that she's in the grip of a heavy crush on me. She's also at a vulnerable age. The more I try to talk to her, to handle the situation tactfully, the more convinced she becomes that she'll eventually…" He paused and shook his head.

"The kindest, the best way, to convince her that she's wrong, that it's time for her to get on with her life, concentrate on her studies, develop a real relationship with someone who will return her feelings, is for her to be convinced that there's someone else in my life. Don't you agree?"

Tullah eyed him narrowly. What he was saying *did* make sense, she had to admit, and from what she had seen of Louise she was also forced to admit that far from being the timid, shrinking person she had imagined, Louise was patently quite capable of stubbornly clinging to her determination to make Saul react sexually to her and, quite probably, the only thing that would put her off was some concrete evidence that there was someone else in Saul's life.

"*Someone* else," she agreed carefully and thoughtfully, "but not me."

"But you're the perfect choice, the obvious choice," Saul insisted. "She's already aware of the fact that you exist, she's seen you here in my home..." He paused and added softly, "In my bed."

Hot colour flared in Tullah's face. "This is *not* your bed," she denied.

But Saul ignored her and continued firmly, "Meg has, I understand, informed her that I undressed you and put you to bed—" he ignored Tullah's outraged, angry gasp "—and it seems to me that she'd already decided exactly what kind of relationship we had even before she tried to threaten you with her own imagined position in my life."

"*We* do not *have* a relationship," Tullah argued.

"We *could* have," Saul coaxed, adding dryly, "*You* were the one who was so concerned about her moral welfare, about the danger to her if she remained infatuated with me. I should have thought you'd have jumped at the chance to help protect her."

Tullah opened her mouth and then closed it

again. He was right, of course, but… "That was when I thought that you…" She stopped.

"When you thought what? That I was taking advantage of her vulnerability? It isn't always the older man who's the instigator, you know, Tullah. There are, I know, some men who do deliberately set out to satisfy their own egos selfishly and, in my opinion, totally unforgivably, preying on their innocent and susceptible young victims, but there are exceptions, cases where…" Saul paused. "He hurt you very much, didn't he?"

"What!" Tullah stiffened defensively before stammering, "How…how did you know…who told you…?"

"Olivia happened to mention a little of your history to me," Saul told her gently, "but it wasn't very hard to guess that there must have been some pain in your past. What happened?"

Tullah tried to resist the gentler note in his voice and found she could not. "He was a friend of the family…my father…and after my parents divorced…" She lowered her head and bit her lip. "He seemed so kind, so caring…. He was just someone I thought of as a friend at first but then we became closer. He said that he loved me…that he'd been waiting for me to grow up. He said we'd always be together, that..."

To her chagrin, she could feel her emotions threatening to overwhelm her. What on earth was she doing, letting Saul Crighton, of all people, see her like this, so vulnerable...so...so...? She'd never talked to *anyone* about exactly how foolish she'd been...how...how stupid. And to talk about it now to Saul...

"Do you love him still?"

Saul's question stunned her. She lifted her head and looked at him. "*Love* him? No, of course I don't. I don't think I ever really did. I think I was only in love with the idea of being in love. I just wanted to feel that I was loved...needed...."

"You needed help, compassion, understanding and, most of all, someone wise enough to recognise what you were going through and why," Saul told her tenderly. "Just as Louise does now."

Their eyes met.

"We can't pretend that we're...that we're involved," she protested, but she knew her voice was losing its conviction. "Are you really serious?" she asked him when he simply looked at her. "Do you really think Louise will be convinced just because she's seen...because...?"

"Yes, I *am* serious," Saul responded, "and since it worked for Luke—in more ways than one… Lucky man," he added half-whimsically.

"What worked for Luke?" she questioned him, confused.

But he simply shook his head and smiled at her, saying, "Trust me, Tullah, it will all work out for the best, I promise."

And then, before Tullah could stop him, he leaned forward and took her in his arms, dropping a very firm kiss on her surprised mouth. A kiss that seemed disturbingly familiar, just like the warm, hard feel of his mouth. So familiar, in fact, that she might actually have previously kissed him and not just dreamt of doing it.

As she pulled herself away from him, she demanded shakily, "What was that for? I…"

"That," Saul informed her, "was to seal our bargain, but this…"

Whilst her eyes widened in shock, Saul cupped her face in his hands, his eyes looking deeply into hers, mesmerising her almost, before he slowly studied her still-parted mouth and then…

Too late, Tullah struggled to break free, to protest what he was doing, but his mouth was already touching hers, caressing hers, and her heart was ricocheting off her chest wall as though it was made of rubber.

How was it possible for her to have dreamt so acutely of Saul's kiss? This intense sensuality simply could not exist and could only be a product of her own imagination, her own fevered dream-induced longings—not for him.... No, never that. No, those longings couldn't possibly have been for Saul. *He* had just been a convenient peg to hang them on, so to speak.

And it was all the fault of the wretched dream that she was now, instead of pushing him away, actually having to fight the urge to wrap her arms around him, lie back on her pillows and subtly incite him to do far, far more than just kiss her.

She wanted him to... She wanted him to... With a small start she realised that either she had spoken her desire out loud or Saul had read her mind because suddenly the pressure of his kiss had deepened and beneath the bedclothes she could feel his hands caressing her naked body, roaming sensuously over her skin before finally capturing her breasts and teasing the already erect crests with his fingertips whilst she moaned in helpless pleasure beneath his mouth.

She wanted him so much. Too much!

As though he sensed her hesitation and ambivalence, his tantalising caresses slowly ceased. Tullah could feel him watching her…waiting.

For what? Permission to torment her still further?

As her body tensed, she felt him withdraw his hands, leaving her on edge, aching…wanting….

"And what was that supposed to be for?" Tullah demanded croakily when Saul had finally completed his leisurely exploration of her mouth. How she had managed to resist his tempting invitations to her to do the same to him, she really did not know, and now in an attempt to regain some kind of control over a situation that, if she was honest with herself, was rapidly escalating way, way out of her control, she struggled to put a safe distance between them and look sternly disapproving—an act she felt was somewhat hampered by the fact that her hair was, no doubt, a wild, tousled cloud of curls and she was having to clutch the bedclothes around her to conceal her body.

"*That* was for me," Saul admitted outrageously, leaving her with no further ammunition to fire at him.

She only managed to demand rather weakly, "And just how long is this supposed relationship of ours going to have to last? Because I—"

"Not that long. Louise will be going back to university at the end of September," he mused, "so I should—"

"September?" Tullah gasped. "But that's some months away. I...we can't...I can't..."

"Think of it as a noble sacrifice you're making for the benefit of a fellow member of your sex," Saul teased her. "That should help the time to go faster."

"Louise will never accept it," Tullah protested. "We don't look like—"

"Lovers," Saul supplied helpfully for her. "Then we'll just have to find a way of making sure that we do, won't we? Don't worry about it," he advised her.

"It won't work," Tullah objected, stubbornly shaking her head, but Saul only laughed.

"We'll *make* it work," he told her. "Wait and see."

CHAPTER TEN

"WELL, you're a dark horse, I must say," Olivia told Tullah dryly. "You and Saul... And there was I, hoping to get you interested in James, when all the time... I thought you were totally anti Saul. You said—"

"I know, I know," Tullah agreed apologetically.

She had known how difficult this particular interview was going to be. She'd been dreading having to face Olivia and the questions she was bound to want to ask, and had said as much to Saul, who had simply frowned for a moment and then offered to do any explaining for her.

"Cower away behind you like some frail Victorian heroine?" Tullah had demanded witheringly. "Certainly not. I don't want or need you to hide behind, Saul, or to run to for protection. I'm simply trying to point out the problems this... this situation you've created is going to cause. Olivia is my friend. She's going to wonder why on earth I haven't said anything to her and she's also..." She paused and bit her lip.

"She's also what?" Saul had encouraged.

They had been standing in his kitchen at the time. Somehow or other he had succeeded in persuading her that, although she was over her migraine, there was no point in her returning home until they had thoroughly discussed their new roles as a couple. One thing had led to another, and before she had known where she was, she had been helping to prepare supper and then get the children to bed, which included reading them all a story. Of course Saul had then insisted she couldn't leave until she had had something to drink, and in the end since it was so late, she had reluctantly conceded that she might as well stay the night, especially since this could only add gravity and conviction to their "plan'.

It had been whilst they had been drinking the nightcap cup of chocolate Saul had made them both that she had broached the subject of his family's reaction to their "news' and more specifically Olivia's.

"Well, you do have...have had, a rather special relationship with her," she had felt compelled to point out, "and she's bound to think, to feel..."

"We are cousins yes, and good friends, too, close friends," Saul had agreed, starting to frown. "But since we're supposed to have fallen intensely and passionately in love during our trip to The Hague, I don't see how there is any way I could have informed Olivia of our relationship before it was supposed to have happened, and in fact—"

"That isn't what I meant," Tullah had interrupted him crossly, shaking her head.

Did he have to be so obtuse, or did he simply think that she didn't know what the situation had once been between him and Olivia?

"You and Olivia were once more than…than just cousins, or even good friends," she reminded him pointedly, "and she might think—"

"Now just a minute," Saul had stopped her grimly. "There was a time when I did rather foolishly believe that the slight crush Olivia and I had had on one another when both of us were too young for it to be taken any further *could* be fanned into something more meaningful and adult, but that was…" He stopped and frowned, shaking his head, then asked her, "Have you discussed this with Olivia?"

"Not…not in any great detail," Tullah admitted. "After all, it isn't really any of my business and—"

"So Olivia hasn't said anything to you about—"

"Olivia hasn't said anything," Tullah cut across him. "If you must know, I doubt I would ever have guessed that there had been anything between you if I hadn't overheard some of Olivia's guests talking about the two of you at Olivia and Caspar's wedding. And then Max confirmed it."

"Talking about *us*...? What were they saying?" Saul had demanded, putting down his cup and coming to stand determinedly in front of Tullah so that there was no way she could avoid answering his questions. His folded-arm stance as he leaned back against the kitchen table made him appear not so much threatening as calmly resolved to drag every single word she had heard out of her, even if it took all night.

"They said..." Tullah took a deep breath and forced herself to meet his eyes. "They said that it was no wonder your marriage had broken up and that you had been unfaithful to your wife with Olivia and nearly caused her and Caspar to break up into the bargain. They also mentioned the fact that Louise had apparently taken Olivia's place in your…your affections."

"What!" Saul grated, demanding, "Who were these people? Describe them to me."

"I don't know," Tullah told him. "They were just two women. I doubt if I would ever recognise them if I saw them again," she answered truthfully.

"But you remembered what they said—and believed it. You actually thought…" He turned round and leaned his hands on the table, keeping his back to her. "Olivia and I have always been close and, yes, there was a time when I did think… Hillary, my wife, was the one who broke our marriage vows, not me, and *she* was also the one who tried to come between Caspar and Olivia, but fortunately Caspar…

"And as for Louise…she was virtually a child still when Olivia and Caspar got married. A child of sixteen… Max has his own axe to grind, of course. His marriage is far from stable, and even if it was, Max is the kind of person who enjoys stirring up trouble." He spaced the words out carefully and slowly as he turned round to confront her. "I was a man of thirty-five going on thirty-six. Have you any idea what it would have made me, if I'd…?"

Tullah had had to bite down hard on her bottom lip to stop its betraying wobble.

"I was fifteen when my parents divorced," she told him huskily. "My…John was nearly forty, but that didn't stop *him*."

She stopped and closed her eyes against the tears she could feel threatening to fall and then to her shock felt herself being propelled roughly into Saul's arms. They closed firmly around her, one of his hands rubbing her back in the same comforting way an adult might console a small child whilst the other held her tear-damp face against the solid warmth of his shoulder as she tried to control the sobs she could feel shaking her whole body.

"I'm sorry. I'm sorry," she managed to hiccup. "I…"

"So am I," she heard Saul's voice rumbling against her. "Hellish sorry that I can't get my hands on him, whoever he is, *wherever* he is, and show just what I think of a man who does to a naïve, trusting child what he did to you. My God, he should be…"

The warm, protective proximity of his body,

the way he was holding her, felt so comforting and reassuring that it came as a shock to discover entwined with her natural response to *those* things, an unexpected and almost painfully sharp twist of physical desire, a need to have him hold her, not just protectively as he might have done a child, but with the sensual pleasure of a man for a woman he very much wanted. Instinctively she moved closer to him, seeking, enticing, some sign that he was as aware of her as a woman as she was of him as a man, subconsciously wanting to prove her femininity and to test his masculinity, and when his body immediately hardened against her, the fierce thrill of shock that brought her skin out in a rash of goose bumps had nothing to do with anger or fear.

Whilst her mind warned her that she was playing a dangerous game, her emotions urged her to give in to the temptation to respond to the silent message of his body language with a response that was equally eloquent.

It was such a heady blend of powerful emotions and sensations to feel at once both protected and comforted and desired. Too heady for her, she admitted, recognising the danger she was setting up for herself. Reluctantly she eased herself away from him. For a moment she thought he was going to protest, to draw her closer, but even as she fought the temptation to give in he was gently allowing her the space she had put between them.

"I was just as much to blame," Tullah told him quietly. "I knew…I wanted—"

"You wanted someone to take your father's place," Saul interrupted her grimly. "You wanted someone to comfort and reassure you, someone to *love* you. You wanted your father, Tullah, and what you got… And you thought that I…that Louise…" Tullah started to tremble as she heard the note of anger in his voice, but to her surprise, instead of voicing it, he simply said quietly, "Well, in the circumstances I suppose I can't blame you. But I hope you know that I would never, *could* never…"

"Yes. Yes, I do," Tullah agreed, swallowing hard as she added tiredly, "After all, that's why you're going to all this trouble, isn't it? Pretending that you and I…"

They never finished their conversation because Jemima had suddenly arrived downstairs saying that she couldn't sleep.

* * *

"You and Saul," Olivia repeated, wondering. "I never even guessed."

"I know…it came as something of a shock to me, as well," Tullah told her quite honestly.

"Mmm…well, Louise isn't too pleased," Olivia warned her. "Jenny was telling me that she's claiming that you've forced your way into Saul's life and his bed and—"

"She what? On the contrary, she couldn't be more wrong," Tullah informed Olivia vigorously.

"Well, Jenny's pleased, at any rate," Olivia went on to advise her. "She's hoping that now she knows that Saul is out of reach, Louise will finally come to her senses and outgrow her crush on him."

"Don't we all," Tullah muttered piously under her breath.

"It's a pity you can't announce the engagement at the Masquerade Ball," Olivia continued. "It would be such a marvellous setting and you look so wonderful in your dress. Have you shown it to Saul, by the way? I haven't shown Caspar mine. I want to keep it a surprise."

"What engagement?" Tullah demanded nervously. "We haven't—"

"No…I know. Saul said that you both felt you

wanted to wait to make a public announcement until after Hugh and Ann get back and that you'd said you wanted to keep the whole thing very low profile until the children had had a chance to get used to the idea of your being around. Mind you, I rather think they're a couple of steps ahead of you there. Meg told me the other day that she's going to be a bridesmaid when Tullah and Daddy '"get married' and that you're going to be her special new mummy."

"What!" Tullah gasped. "We haven't…I haven't…"

That was one point she had been very determined about. There was no way, she had informed Saul, that she was going to allow the children to be hurt by what they were doing.

To her astonishment, Saul's response had been to take her in his arms and tell her in a voice thick with emotion, "Tullah. Tullah, I could love you just for that alone. They *won't* be hurt," he had assured her. "I'll make sure of that."

It was only later that she realised exactly what he had said. What he had said, but hardly, of course, what he had meant. She must remember, she had told herself firmly, that he'd used the word "could' meaning it was possible for him to love her. But quite patently it wasn't, which was just as well because she certainly did not, could not, love him. Could she?

"It's fortunate that Saul and you have good jobs," Olivia said, chuckling, apparently oblivious to Tullah's shock. "There's obviously going to be a large family to support. Half a dozen at least, I would guess, and—"

"What?" Tullah squeaked in protest. "Olivia… we aren't—"

"It's all right. It's all right," Olivia soothed her. "I *do* understand. But you were made for motherhood, Tullah. The children already adore you and I'll bet Saul just can't wait to see you with a baby…*his* baby in your arms. He's that kind of man. He loves children, he always has."

"He…he does…?" Tullah exclaimed weakly, too bemused by the unexpectedly tempting vision Olivia had just given of her lying in bed holding her…*their* newborn child whilst Saul and the other three children looked lovingly on to point out to Olivia the real purpose behind her "relationship' with Saul.

After all, there could be no harm in Olivia knowing the truth, but it seemed that far from guessing that the sudden discovery of their "love' for one another was a fiction, Olivia was all too obviously delighted with the way things had turned out, or rather the way she imagined things had turned out. Listening to her, Tullah cravenly acknowledged that foolish though it might be of her, she simply couldn't resist allowing herself the dangerous pleasure of going along with Olivia's enthusiasm, of pretending to herself as well as Olivia that she and Saul had a future together.

She would, of course, correct Olivia's misapprehension just as soon as she could find a suitable opportunity to do so, she assured herself firmly.

Good heavens, what on earth was happening to her? She wasn't…she didn't…she hadn't… She was a career girl and not…

"We could always use your expertise in the practice if you ever felt like going back to work," Olivia was continuing. "In fact, we're getting so busy we've already asked Bobbie about taking on some part-time work and we're actually having to advertise for a qualified full-time solicitor."

"Olivia," Tullah felt bound to tell her friend, "Saul and I haven't even… We've barely… We haven't even *talked* about…about the future or having a family," she finally managed to say truthfully.

"It isn't talking that produces families, babies," Olivia pointed out wickedly. "Mark my words," she added sagely, "by this time next year you and Saul—"

"By this time next year Tullah and Saul will what?" Caspar asked, thankfully appearing from his study to end what for Tullah was becoming an increasingly hazardous conversation.

"Never you mind," Olivia warned her husband. "And don't forget that you and Saul and Jon are due to go and try your costumes on tomorrow." When he groaned, she reminded him, "The ball *is* this weekend, Cas—"

"I know, I know," he agreed. "How could I not when you haven't talked about anything else for the past few weeks, well, that and Tullah and Saul?"

Thankfully Tullah used the excuse of having some shopping to do to escape before Olivia could ask her any more questions.

She and Saul married, with a family, children… a baby…babies of their own. Oh, it was completely impossible, of course, and Olivia would be the first to say so herself if she knew what the real situation was. Yes, it was totally impossible.

Totally and completely, and *she* had better just remember that because if she didn't…

If she didn't and she was foolish enough to get carried away with this ridiculous fiction Saul had concocted that they were a couple… But, of course, she wasn't foolish at all, was she?

She was grateful that the proximity of the Masquerade Ball, which was now only a few days away, took at least some of the curiosity value and heat out of their own situation.

What had amazed her, though, was how quickly gossip could spread in a small community. Within a couple of days of her giving her reluctant agreement to Saul's scheme, several of her work colleagues had made reference to her relationship with Saul.

The general impression she had received from her female colleagues, at least, was that she was the subject of their amicably good-natured envy.

"You lucky thing, he's gorgeous, a real hunk and nice besides," one of the women had groaned enviously.

Tullah had laughed and agreed and then had been warily conscious of just how easy she was finding it to pretend that she was in love with Saul. Too easy?

* * *

"I'm not going to let her take Saul away from me," Louise declared passionately as she paced the floor of the bedroom she shared with her twin who was now also back from college.

"She already has," Katie observed pragmatically. "You only want him because you can't have him. By the way, have you finished that course work yet?" she asked. "You know that Professor Simmonds said—"

Louise scowled horribly and mimicked her sister. "Professor Simmonds. He's a bore. What does he know?"

"Enough to have you sent down if you miss any more lectures and don't catch up with your work," Katie warned her. "He's on to us, Lou. He knows that I've been standing in for you at some of his lectures. He even called me Katherine last week and told me he wants to see you and you're to come with all your work up to date."

Louise's scowl deepened. "Interfering old busybody."

"He's not old," Katie protested. "He's one of the youngest professors they've ever had and he's not interfering either. You're supposed to be one of his students and if you keep on missing your tutorials…"

"You agreed that you'd do that for me."

"No, I didn't. You said I *had* to. I haven't got time, Lou. I've got my own course work to do. You know how upset Mum and Dad are going to be if you get kicked out of university. They'll think that Uncle David is coming out in you as well as Max."

Louise made a face at this reference. "Well, he isn't. I'm not a bit like Uncle David."

"Yes, you are," Katie contradicted her. "Once you get an idea in your head, it's like someone's put blinkers on you. You can't *make* another person love you, and if you could, the person you should be hoping feels that emotion for you right now is Professor Simmonds. You need his love much more than you do Saul's... *Uncle* Saul's," she stressed firmly. "You've really got to get down to some work, Lou," she warned her sister seriously.

"Oh, for heaven's sake, don't start on that again. And Saul's not an *uncle*," Louise said irritably. "All right, so I'll do the course work. Satisfied?"

But it wasn't the work she was thinking about half an hour later after Katie had gone out. There must be some way she could make Saul see how wrong this Tullah was for him and how right she was. And she would find it. Oh yes, she would find it.

CHAPTER ELEVEN

A LITTLE nervously, Tullah smoothed down the heavy brocade of her hired gown. The rich crimson and gold of her outfit suited her colouring to perfection, the mask that went with it giving her half-hidden features a mysterious allure.

At Saul's suggestion, he was coming to pick her up to take her to the Ball. "The girls want to see you in your outfit," he had told Tullah. "Especially Jem."

All the children were to spend the night at Queensmead. There was more than enough room for them there, Olivia had announced when Louise's twin, Katie, had offered to babysit. "You'll like her," Olivia had told Tullah. "She's not a bit like Louise. In fact, although physically they look exactly alike, temperamentally they couldn't be more different."

Tullah and Saul had planned to drop off his three children at Queensmead on their way to the Ball.

"Have you met Livvy's grandfather yet?" Saul had asked Tullah, and when she had shaken her head, he had given her a wry smile. "Well, he's quite a character, very much of the old school. The honour and integrity of the "'family' are very important to him. He and my father are half-brothers. Their father married twice and there's quite an age gap between Olivia's grandfather and my father. They've never been particularly close. Ben, Olivia's grandfather, isn't someone who's easy to get close to, and reading between the lines, I suspect that he feels that my father, as the youngest child and with a mother who came from a pretty well-to-do background, was more favoured by fortune than he was himself. Ben was actually a sole-surviving twin and from all accounts he grew up knowing his father would never get over the loss of his first born son and maybe even blamed Ben for it.

"Oh, poor man," Tullah had sympathised immediately. "How sad."

"Yes, in many ways I think his life has been," Saul had agreed pensively. "And yet until now I never really saw it like that and tended to think of him as someone awkward and not a little bloody-minded. I've certainly always been thankful that

I'm my father's son and not his. Jon didn't have a very easy time of it when he was growing up. David was always very much the apple of his father's eye and poor Jon was cast very much in *his* shadow."

"David, that's Olivia's father, isn't it?" Tullah had queried interestedly.

"Yes," Saul had affirmed. "He disappeared in the aftermath of a heart attack—no one knows where or why, although I suspect..." He had stopped abruptly, and sensitively Tullah hadn't pressed him.

She suspected from little remarks that Olivia had dropped the odd time about her parents, and specifically her father, that there were flaws in his personality, which meant that Olivia was not entirely sorry that he was no longer a part of their lives.

"Even as a child I was always much closer to Jenny and Jon," she had admitted to Tullah on one occasion. "Gramps often used to say that Max should have been David's son and me Jon's daughter."

Tullah had only met Max and his long-suffering, patient, rather quiet wife, Madeleine, a couple of times, and she had very quickly formed the opinion that Max was a risk taker, a man who enjoyed living life on the edge and one who was without the saving grace of sensitivity or kindness. He certainly wasn't very kind to his wife, if the rumours she had heard about his roving eye and infidelity were to be believed.

She tensed as she heard Saul draw up outside, her heart starting to beat rather too fast. It must be the constricting corset that went with the gown that was causing her shortness of breath, she decided crossly as she made her way downstairs, one of the penalties that went with the miraculously small waist its tight lacing had achieved, and nothing whatsoever to do with Saul's arrival, of course. Of course!

Like her, Saul was already dressed in his costume, and as she opened the door to him, Tullah felt her breath catch in her throat.

Realistically there could have been something almost ridiculous and foppish about a twentieth-century male dressed in knee-breeches, white stockings, a heavy brocaded coat and carrying a cane and tricorn hat, but what her senses were telling her was something very different indeed.

Georgette Heyer had an awful lot to answer for, Tullah decided shakily as her heartbeat picked up and she discovered she was perilously close to what her eighteenth-century equivalent would probably have termed a swoon and what she forthrightly told herself was simply an ill-advised and illogical surge of lust.

"I should be wearing a wig, but it made me itch unbearably and so I ditched it," she heard Saul telling her wryly as she studied him. "How the devil anyone lived anything like a normal life dressed in these things I'll never know."

"I…I don't expect they did," Tullah managed to respond dizzily. "I expect, like us, they wore more practical things for day-to-day living."

She had quickly pulled on the matching cloak that covered her costume before going downstairs, suddenly shy and self-conscious about letting Saul see her, and hurried now to the door.

"We mustn't be late," she told him.

"We won't be," Saul responded calmly, adding, "Where's your case? I'll put it in the boot."

Her case… Of course, she had left it upstairs! It had been Olivia's innocent comment about the fact that she and Saul would no doubt be taking full advantage of the rare absence of the children overnight at Queensmead that had led to Saul telling her that it would look odd if, after the

Ball, she insisted on returning home alone, and so reluctantly she had conceded that he was right and agreed to stay overnight at Saul's house and go with him in the morning to collect the children and take part in the family lunch Jenny was planning for all of them at Queensmead.

"It's…it's upstairs," she told him falteringly. "I'll go and—"

"No, you stay here. I'll get it," Saul told her, moving far more easily up the narrow stairs than she could have done with her full, stiff, paniered skirts. The costume did extraordinary things to her figure, which she wasn't quite sure she felt totally comfortable about. Olivia had laughed when she demurred and expressed her doubts about a bodice so tight that it made her waist look tiny enough to be easily spanned by a man's hands and her breasts firm and voluptuously rounded.

"You're lucky," she had told Tullah. "I suspect I'm going to need a little help from some judicious padding to achieve the authentic eighteenth-century round-breasted look. "I never realised you had a mole there," she had added wickedly, laughing again when Tullah tried to pull up the lace edging on her bodice to conceal the small dark mole prettily and provocatively positioned where normally the only person other than herself to see it would be a lover.

Upstairs in Tullah's bedroom, Saul spotted the suitcase immediately. The bedroom itself was commendably neat and tidy and yet at the same time irrepressibly feminine, a pair of satin mules half-hidden beneath the bed, a small enamelled pot full of lipsticks on the dressing table, the scent of Tullah's perfume hanging on the air. He glanced at the bed and then looked away.

He had protested that the satin knee-breeches that went with his costume were a little on the tight side but had been told that that was the style of the period. Style or not, it was damned uncomfortable when Tullah was around and he… Quickly he picked up her suitcase and headed for the door.

The bodice of her dress quite definitely was too tight, Tullah decided as she watched Saul coming back downstairs and discovered that she was having difficulty drawing breath. Nothing to do with the fact that the tight style of his costume revealed that Saul had exceedingly powerful thighs and that… Blushing, she looked away as she realised just what directions her thoughts were taking.

She would be glad when these next few weeks were over and Louise was safely back at university and this relationship could be brought to an end, she decided as she got into the front seat of Saul's car and turned round to greet the children who were seated in the back.

"What on earth is that?" Katie demanded, staring uneasily at her sister.

"What does it look like?" Louise replied, pirouetting in front of their shared bedroom mirror. "It's an eighteenth century ball gown."

"Yes, but where did you get it and what are you doing with it on? You aren't invited to the masquerade."

"Mmm..." Louise murmured absently frowning, as she pulled the front of her gown down a little farther and turned sideways to study the effect.

"You haven't got a ticket," Katie continued. "You can't go—"

"Who's going to stop me?" Louise asked her, laughing.

"You don't mean you're going to gatecrash? You

can't," Katie protested, appalled. "What if the parents find out and—"

"They won't," Louise assured her. "Look," she told her twin, reaching into the large box on the bedroom floor. "Once I put this mask on, no one will recognise me!"

Katie was forced to admit that she was right but she still felt uneasily conscious that she ought to dissuade Louise from what she planned to do.

"Why do you want to go?" she asked her.

Louise raised her eyebrows. "Why do you think? Saul will be there."

"He'll be there with Tullah," Katie reminded her. "You shouldn't be doing this."

"Oh no? And who's going to stop me? Your precious Professor Simmonds?"

"He's not my professor, he's yours," Katie reminded her, adding, "Well, he's your tutor anyway. Oh, Louise, have you thought how upset Mum and Dad will be if—"

"They won't be upset because they won't *know*," Louise told her firmly, adding fiercely. "I've got to do something to show Saul what a fool he's being. I just need a chance to show him. Isn't it time you left for Queensmead to do your babysitting?"

"Lou come with me instead," Katie begged, but Louise simply shook her head.

"No," she told her heatedly. "I've made up my mind."

"Right, are we all ready...?" Olivia demanded.

They had arrived at Queensmead fifteen minutes or so earlier and the children were all tucked up safely in their respective beds.

Tullah had been introduced to Olivia's grandfather, a spare, elderly man who had eyed her piercingly and harrumphed that Saul was a damn lucky man before announcing that he was going to spend the evening in his study and that he didn't want to be disturbed.

Tullah had gone upstairs with Olivia to help settle the children and at Meg's urging had removed the cloak to show them her gown. Meg's eyes had rounded in awe as she stared at her, but it had been the expression on Jemima's face as she hesitantly touched the rich fabric of her costume that had brought a sharp pang of emotion to Tullah, and acting on instinct, she had held out her arms to the older girl and hugged her tightly as Jemima choked out, "You look so beautiful. I wish I was pretty."

"You are…you *are*," Tullah had told her feelingly.

"No, I'm not," Jemima had denied. "My mother used to say that I was the plainest child she'd ever seen."

Tullah's breath had caught in her throat at the pain and loss she could hear in Jemima's voice. How could Saul's ex-wife, no matter how difficult her own life might have been at the time, no matter how unhappy the marriage might have been making her feel, have said something so cruel and so untrue to her own child?

"If that's what she said, then I think that your mother must have needed glasses," Tullah had told her gently. "Because you most certainly are not plain."

"You're only saying that because I look like Dad and you love him," the child had countered sadly.

"Oh, Jemima." Tullah had almost wept as she hugged her even closer. "That simply isn't true. You're not plain, I promise you. You're not plain at all. On the contrary, I strongly suspect you are going to grow up to be a real heartbreaker."

Poor little girl, Tullah had reflected five minutes later as she and Olivia went back downstairs. How could her mother have said that to her, especially when it quite patently wasn't true?

Was that perhaps the reason why Jemima was sometimes so quiet and withdrawn, why she seemed to want to wear such dull, almost ugly clothes? If so, then in future she was going to make sure that the girl was encouraged to know that she was attractive and that she deserved to wear pretty, brightly coloured clothes, and it might be as well, too, if she and Saul postponed starting a family of their own until she felt a bit more confident about herself. The last thing Tullah wanted to do was to make her feel even more insecure.

Abruptly Tullah tensed. What on earth was she doing...what on earth was she thinking? She and Saul weren't going to *have* a family. She didn't have any role to play in Jemima's life. Was she going completely crazy?

Although for the most part, the events of the evening were being held in the open air, a marquee had been erected to serve as a cloakroom, and as Olivia pointed out to Tullah when they arrived, it was certainly warm enough for them to be able to dispense with their cloaks.

"The organisers have been lucky with the weather. It's a lovely night." As they collected their tickets, she remarked, "These masks are a clever idea, don't you think? They really do provide an effective disguise, although not in your case," she added teasingly, with a meaningful glance in the direction of Tullah's bosom. "I doubt very much that Saul will have any difficulty in recognising you. Because of your mole, I meant," she added straight-faced as Tullah shot her a suspicious look.

She was still laughing when they rejoined the men, and to Tullah's embarrassment, Caspar asked to be included in the joke.

Saul was talking to someone and had his back to them and only turned round when Olivia was part way through her explanation. As he saw Tullah, he seemed to freeze for a second, his whole body tensing as he stood and looked at her.

Then Olivia was exhorting, "Saul, it's true, isn't it? Even with her mask on, you'd recognise Tullah, thanks to her tell-tale mole?"

Laughing again, she pointed to the small dark mark on Tullah's left breast whilst Tullah instinctively raised her mask to her face to hide its hot scorch of mortified colour.

"I could recognise her even without it," she heard Saul responding quietly to Olivia. "But

I agree, it is rather eye…catching," and then to Olivia's consternation, he added throatily, "and very, very kissable."

"Oh, poor Tullah, now we have embarrassed her," Olivia teased as Tullah made a small, agonized sound beneath her breath. "James is supposed to be coming. I wonder if he's here yet," Olivia commented.

"Close to five hundred people have been invited," Saul warned her. "So even if he is here, we might not actually see him."

"Don't the gardens look wonderful?" Olivia enthused.

"Very pretty," Caspar agreed imperturbably, "although I suspect in the eighteenth century they would have been lit with pitch torches instead of fake electric ones."

Olivia pouted at him. "Trust you…but I suppose the electric ones are much safer. I love the way they've made those pretty little booths and pavilions. Oh, look at that," she exclaimed excitedly as a troupe of acrobats leaped and somersaulted their way past them followed by a fire-eater. "Oh, Saul, it's wonderful. I've never seen anything like it," she admitted.

Neither had Tullah and she was just as bemused and awestruck by their surroundings as Olivia.

In the distance they could see the magnificent backdrop of the hall itself, out of bounds to their party along with the private gardens that surrounded it. Below them, on the artificial canal that fed the pretty lake with its grotto and temple, brightly painted gondolas complete with gondoliers bobbed on the placid water.

Tullah smiled as she listened to the sound of the quartet striking up on the edge of the dance floor several yards away.

"Shall we take a stroll?" Saul suggested, offering Tullah his arm in courtly style.

"Watch it, you two," Olivia warned them as Tullah moved closer to Saul. "Just remember that since you're not yet formally betrothed, you really shouldn't be alone together without a chaperon."

"Milady is perfectly safe with me," Saul responded drolly, "and as for a chaperon, do we not have the bright light of the moon to guard and protect her? Although, I must admit, faced with such beauty… such temptation…"

Tullah tried to share the others' laughter, but

there was an extraordinary tight sensation in her chest, a hopeless yearning…a need.

"I don't really feel like dancing," she lied, pulling away from Saul. "I'm…I'm thirsty. I wonder where we can get a drink."

"I'll go and get you something. What would you like?" Saul spoke politely, but rather distantly, Tullah thought.

Ten minutes later when Saul returned with Tullah's drink, Olivia and Caspar were dancing, and when Saul was sidetracked by one of the members of the Board who wanted to discuss something with him, Tullah decided that she might as well explore and enjoy the surroundings on her own. The sight of a couple kissing passionately in the shadows made her heart ache enviously.

She was being ridiculous, she chided herself. She *wasn't* in love with Saul, how could she be? Just because she had discovered that he wasn't the man she had initially assumed him to be didn't mean that she had to go from one extreme to the other and exchange hate for love.

"Excuse me…?" Tullah frowned as a masked woman approached her.

"It's my friend," the other woman told her

urgently. “She’s fallen and hurt herself. I wonder if you could help me.”

As she spoke, she was already tugging Tullah in the direction of the topiary maze that was a famous feature of the estate’s gardens and a place Tullah had assumed was out of bounds to the partygoers, but the other woman was walking so fast, almost running, in fact, that it was difficult enough for Tullah to keep pace with her and manage her own awkward skirts without finding the breath to question her. The other woman’s urgency and alarm had also communicated itself to Tullah so that she only hesitated fractionally before allowing herself to be pulled into the entrance to the maze.

She asked anxiously, “What’s happened to your friend? If she’s fallen and hurt herself, shouldn’t we get some kind of professional help for her? There’s a first-aid tent and—”

“No, there isn’t time for that. She’s afraid, you see. She didn’t want me to leave her. It’s very dark in the maze and she hates the dark....”

There was a certain degree of rather chilling relish in the other woman’s voice as she made this comment and Tullah had an odd and disturbing conviction that she knew her although she couldn't quite place her husky voice.

"It's this way," she directed Tullah, darting down one of the long green tunnels that, as she had stated, were rather dark and disturbingly shadowed at this time of night.

It was just as well *she* knew where she was going, Tullah acknowledged, because she could certainly never have found her way to wherever it was they were heading. They had taken so many turns that she was confused already. She started to say as much, then gave a shocked gasp as, totally unexpectedly, her companion released her and darted through a space in the green wall. But when Tullah followed her through it, there was no sign of her, the shadowy green avenue now deserted.

Assuming that her companion had not realised that she was missing, Tullah waited for her to reappear. When she did not do so after several minutes, Tullah's original confusion and irritation began to turn to anger.

What was going on? Was someone, one of her colleagues perhaps, playing some kind of practical joke on her? If so, it wasn't a particularly pleasant one. It was chilly inside the maze and very dark and Tullah was already beginning to wish she had her cloak with her.

"All right," she called out firmly, "the joke's over, I give up. Now come out and let's just get out of here."

Silence.

She was not going to panic…yet, Tullah told herself. After all, it should be a simple enough process to retrace her footsteps, shouldn't it? She was beginning to conclude she had been lured in here and then left as some sort of silly prank.

Surely all she had to do was concentrate and try to remember which turns they had taken. The trouble was, though, that because of the speed with which she had been rushed into the maze and the anxiety for the supposed friend who had fallen, she had not paid much attention to the route they had taken, and if she was honest with herself, she had never had much sense of direction. In fact, the other woman had hurried her so much that the small bag she had been carrying must have slipped off her arm at some stage, she realised, because she certainly didn't have it with her now.

She started to shiver and rubbed her arms, trying to banish the goose bumps lifting on her skin. The moon, which had seemed to be shining so brightly earlier, only cast dark shadows here in the maze. The green walls must be at least ten feet high, Tullah reflected, making an effort to subdue her growing panic by visualising them as much smaller, small enough for her to see over. If only… How long was she going to be left here and why?

If this was someone's idea of a practical joke, it was a pretty cruel one. She couldn't think of anyone who disliked her enough to subject her to something like this. Or could she…? She shivered again but not with cold this time. Louise! *That* was why she had thought she recognised the voice. It had been *Louise*. Louise had tricked her into coming to the maze and once there had trapped her inside.

But for what purpose? Sooner or later someone was bound to realise that she was missing. Sooner…or later. How *much* later…and how long before they actually found her?

A small bubble of hysteria welled up in her throat. The maze was off limits to those attending the Ball, she was sure of it. It was the last place anyone would think of looking for her. Her whole body sagged as defeat and weariness overwhelmed her.

* * *

Saul frowned as he surveyed the crowd on the dance floor once again. It was over half an hour now since he had finally shaken off his fellow member of the Board, and although he had searched assiduously for her, he had seen no sign whatsoever of Tullah. Olivia, when asked, had looked surprised to discover that she was not with him; her colleagues from work had shaken their heads and watched curiously as he walked away, suspecting a lovers' tiff.

"Saul!" He scowled as he watched Louise come running towards him, adroitly sidestepping at the last minute so that instead of flinging herself into his arms as she had obviously intended, he was able to hold her off.

"Louise, what are *you* doing here?" he challenged her.

Louise pouted provocatively at him. She *knew* it was provocative because she had been practising it in the mirror. A good many of her fellow male university students had shown her that they found her attractive and asked her out on dates, but there was only one man she was interested in, only one. Saul.

"You haven't said I look nice," she told him, ignoring his question and stepping back to do a small twirl in front of him. She had been pleased with the way the tight-fitting corset had forced her breasts up and out, giving them a fullness and her a cleavage she could not ordinarily boast. Katie had been slightly disapproving when she had seen her.

"If that bodice was pulled any lower you'd be in danger of showing your nipples," she had told her twin forthrightly.

Louise had merely pulled a small face. Saul, though, far from being impressed by the generous amount of flesh she was revealing, barely even gave her the most cursory of looks.

She'd seen the way he'd looked at Tullah, though, earlier in the evening when no one had been aware that she was watching them, hidden away safely behind her mask and making sure she kept to the shadows. But then, men historically *did* have a weakness for that kind of overblown blowziness and breasts that Louise quite frankly thought were just too over the top.

"Looking for someone?" she asked Saul archly, taking advantage of his preoccupation to slide her arm through his and move closer to him.

"Yes…Tullah," Saul replied curtly. "Have you seen her?"

Louise could feel him moving away from her as she tried to lean against him and her angry resentment against Tullah grew, banishing the guilt she had felt when she had run off and left the other woman in the maze. Tullah was not in any real danger, of course. Someone, one of Lord Astlegh's employees, was bound to check the maze at the end of the evening even though it was out of bounds to the revellers and, just in case, she intended to do so herself later, once everyone else was safely out of the way. It was a warm night and Tullah couldn't possibly come to any harm. All Louise had wanted to do was to get her out of the way for a while, to make Saul see that she simply wasn't right for him and now she realised that Saul himself had unwittingly made her task even easier.

Trying both to conceal her triumph and to sound suitably casual, Louise shrugged her shoulders and told him untruthfully, "Yes, as a matter of fact I have—"

"Where?" Saul demanded without allowing her to finish, and for the first time he actually moved towards her, his eyes blazing.

"Er, it must have been about twenty minutes or

so ago," Louise replied glibly. "She was dancing with someone. I—"

"Dancing?" Saul's expression reflected his perplexity. He had been searching the dance floor for quite some time, hoping to see Tullah, but he hadn't seen her dancing.

"Yes…with a tall man wearing a wig," Louise improvised. "They were laughing about something and then they walked off together in the direction of the car park."

"What?" Saul looked thunderous.

This was wonderful. Her plan was working even better than she had hoped, Louise acknowledged as she took advantage of Saul's dropped guard to place her hand possessively on his arm as she moved even closer to him and told him softly, "I'm sorry, Saul, but she and whoever it was did seem…very…friendly. She…"

Caught up by the apparent success of her scheming, Louise was too distracted to notice that out of the corner of his eye, Saul had spotted the pale satin fabric of the bag that she had stuffed into the pocket of her cloak after she realised that Tullah had dropped it. Trapping her foe in the maze and coming between her and Saul was one thing. Allowing her to lose her purse was a very different kind of offence and one she simply didn't have it in her to commit. The purse would be restored to Tullah along with her freedom once Saul had been persuaded that he no longer wanted Tullah in his life.

Mentally busy with her plans, Louise wasn't even aware of Saul reaching forward and removing the purse from her pocket until he demanded sternly, "Where did you get this?"

Louise could feel the hot, guilty colour burning her face.

"Louise," Saul warned her grimly, "I *know* this is Tullah's bag. Now, where did you get it?"

Ten minutes later after he had finally dragged the truth from her, Louise was consigned to Olivia's guardianship. Saul could only shake his head when Olivia asked him uncertainly what was wrong.

"I haven't time to tell you now. Just keep an eye on Louise for me, will you? And as for you, my girl," he admonished Louise harshly, "just think yourself lucky that you're not my child and that I don't have any jurisdiction over you. Because *if* I did... You claim to be a woman, Louise, but your behaviour is that of an irresponsible, immature child and that is exactly how I think of you—as a child—and that is how I will *always* think of you."

Somehow or other Louise managed to hold back the tears she was longing to cry. Suddenly she felt as though she didn't know Saul at all, as though he was a stranger, a stern, authoritarian figure whom she found as unappealing and irritating as her tutor. Her tutor. She could just imagine *his* reaction if he ever found out about tonight. Not that he would ever find out, of course. Fiercely she blinked back her tears. Olivia was watching her with mingled irritation and sympathy.

"Saul's right, you know, Lou," she told her gently. "It *is* time for you to start growing up."

"I *am* grown up," Louise told her flatly and at that moment she realised that it was true; that there was a huge, empty, painful place inside her where her love for Saul had been; that all she wanted to do was to escape from her family and from the scene of her humiliation and most of all from Saul. There was no way she could spend the rest of the summer in Haslewich now. No way at all….

It took Saul ten minutes to reach the maze and once there he didn't hesitate. His father and the present Earl had been contemporaries; as children he and his brother had visited the hall with his parents when they had been staying at Queensmead. They had played in the maze with the Earl's children and Saul, with his quick analytical brain, had quickly mastered the intricacies of the maze's layout.

He only hoped that he could remember it accurately, otherwise he would have to go up to the hall and trust that in the Earl's absence there was someone available who could provide a map of it.

Tullah blinked away angry tears as yet another attempt to find her way out of the maze had led to a dead end.

She was cold and tired and, worst of all, starting to pay much too much attention to the lurid and surely far-fetched images produced by her imagination. There was, after all, no way she could be lost in here long enough to starve to death. Someone obviously clipped these impeccably straight green walls that imprisoned her, and besides, she hadn't gained the impression from Louise that it was her *life* she wanted to end, only her relationship with Saul.

Her relationship with Saul. If only Louise had known the truth.

She closed her eyes. She would just rest for a little while and then she would try again to find her way out.

She tensed as she thought she heard someone, *someone...Saul*, calling her name. So paralysed was she by the huge surge of relief that engulfed her that it was several seconds before she was able to respond and call back.

"Saul...I'm here...here...." she cried out as she started to run down the dark green avenue, propelled more by instinct than logic, by emotion, relief and most of all by the sheer overwhelming need not just to be rescued but to be with Saul.

And then suddenly he was there, emerging out of the darkness to stand at the end of the dark tunnel.

Saul!

Without pausing or hesitating, Tullah ran towards him and flung herself into his arms.

Saul was here, thank God. Thank God! She had known that ultimately someone must miss her and start to look for her. Of course she had, and yet...and yet...

She knew she would have been emotional and

relieved no matter who had rescued her, but the fact that it was *Saul* made it so much more natural and instinctive that she should give in to the emotions that she might otherwise have tried, as an adult, to control. In *Saul's* arms, though, it was easy to allow herself the feeling of relief, the release of tears, the vulnerability of shivering, trembling, clinging shakily to him, abandoning herself totally to his warmth, his presence, his protection.

"Oh, Saul, I'm so glad it's you," she told him in a rush of words, unable to hold them back. "I'm so glad you found me."

"So am I," she heard him responding huskily as though somehow it almost hurt him to speak. "So am I."

Odd how very different it felt, *he* felt, when it was the woman you wanted; the woman you ached for; hungered for; yearned for. The woman you *loved*, whose body you could feel next to your own, Saul recognised as his arms fastened round Tullah. Holding her, rocking her as she sobbed out her shock and relief against his shoulder, he comforted her much as he would have done had she been one of his children.

"Oh, Saul, I thought I was going to be in here

for ever, that I'd never find my way out…that no one would ever know what happened to me," Tullah admitted, too relieved to have him there to care about how vulnerable or foolish he might think her.

In response, Saul's arms tightened round her even harder. "I'd never have let that happen," he told her fiercely. "Even if I'd had to tear out every single damn part of this place with my bare hands."

"I don't think the Earl would have been very pleased about that," Tullah hiccuped, torn between tears and laughter.

"I don't give a damn. All I care about is that I've found you and you're safe. All I care about is *you*," he told her, his voice suddenly rough and very deep.

Uncertainly Tullah looked up at him. "You don't have to play the part of the anxious lover here," she reminded him huskily. "There's only us."

"Who says that I'm playing?" Saul countered.

She felt so very good in his arms and it was just beginning to strike him that so far she had made no move to pull away from him and that was a fact. He looked at her upturned face. The moonlight silvered her skin, her cheek-bones, her jawline so delicate and fragile, the soft curve of her throat and the even softer swell of her breasts.

He took a deep breath and told her, "If you keep on looking at me like that, I'm going to *have* to kiss you…."

Tullah's lips moved as she was forced to swallow but she didn't look away.

"Tullah," Saul warned her rawly as her gaze finally slid from his eyes to his mouth and stayed there.

She had never dreamt that anything could possibly seem so right, so natural, so instinctive and easy and yet at the same time feel so mystical and preordained, so spiritual almost, that it was as though she and Saul were being drawn together by something that was stronger than both of them.

She rocked gently in his arms as he started to kiss her, slowly at first, lingering over the slow fusion of their mouths, his hands sliding into her hair, cupping her face and holding it as though her lips were some aphrodisiacal font he was drinking from. Gradually as he felt her response, her body's soft compliance, his kiss became more intimate, more demanding, as he became more the dominant lover and less the supplicant. A man, her *man*, Tullah recognised as she luxuriated in her recognition of his desire and her own need to respond to it.

"You *know* I love you, don't you?" Saul murmured when he finally released her mouth and tenderly kissed the shadowy hollow between her breasts.

"I… Are you sure?" Tullah asked him hesitantly.

"Aren't you?" Saul countered gently.

Tullah gave him an uncertain look and then admitted, "Yes…" adding in a burst of anxiety, "But I didn't *want* to love you, Saul, and until tonight *you* didn't love me and—"

"What? Of course I loved you. Perhaps not right from the start when I first saw you at Olivia's wedding and again at the christening, although I did try to talk to you." He gave a small shrug. "When I found out you were joining the company and Olivia invited us both to that dinner, I thought…but then you made it plain that I was the last person you'd ever be interested in."

"Because I thought—"

"I *know* what you thought," Saul checked her dryly.

"I'm sorry," Tullah apologised, "but..."

"I know."

"Do you think we'd ever have got together if we hadn't been forced to pretend to be...involved?" she asked him.

"Oh, I think I'd have found a way," Saul assured her softly. "But fortunately I haven't needed to. Luke's ploy worked just as well for me as it did for him."

"Luke's ploy...what do you mean?" Tullah questioned him.

"When Bobbie first arrived in Chester, Luke pretended that he was having a relationship with her to get rid of an ex-girlfriend who was trying to restart a long-dead affair."

"Like you and me with Louise," Tullah murmured as she nestled deeper into the warmth of his arms.

"Mmm...and when fate presented me with the opportunity to do the same thing, I remembered how well it worked for Luke and it ended up with him and Bobbie getting married, so I decided to see if it could work as well for me."

"Do you think we'd ever have really found out how we felt about one another if it hadn't been for tonight, for Louise?" Tullah asked.

"I'm sure of it," Saul told her positively. "I doubt very much that I could have held out much longer against my baser instincts, especially since my body already knows just how good we are together," he whispered before he bent his head and started to kiss her again.

Tullah had to wait until he had finished to demand, "What do you mean? We haven't, we've never..."

"Oh yes, we have," Saul told her with a wicked smile, then bending his head he started to whisper to her exactly what she had said to him the night they'd made love.

Tullah stared at him. "But I thought that was just a dream," she protested.

Saul laughed. "It was no dream," he told her teasingly. "Want me to prove it?"

His hands were already moving over her body, her senses, her sensuality springing hotly to life beneath his touch, her lips parting eagerly as his met the warmth of hers. Her earlier fear, the cold, the discomfort and distress she had suffered, were all but forgotten, and the trembling that convulsed her body as Saul gently eased her breasts free of the constriction of her bodice to slowly stroke and then far more passionately caress them with his mouth had nothing whatsoever to do with the chilly air.

Tullah moaned huskily as her whole body responded to Saul's mouth against her breasts, her head tilting back to expose the smooth column of her throat.

The moonlight turned her body to creamy alabaster and Saul groaned ruefully as he gathered and pressed her up against him, whispering rawly, "Do you know how much I want you right now?"

"I want you, too," Tullah admitted shakily, "but..." She glanced doubtfully at their surroundings.

"I know," Saul agreed. "This is not really the place, and besides, if we don't put in an appearance soon, the others will be sending out a search party for us. So, much as I want to have you all to myself..."

He paused and leaned forward, readjusting her dress, kissing her gently on the mouth and then less gently as he felt her move closer to him, her hands clutching at him as though she was still half-afraid that he might disappear.

"I love you so much, do you *know* that?" he whispered against her mouth emotively as he released her, then added more matter-of-factly. "We'd better get back. Olivia's probably had enough of guarding Louise by now."

"Louise...? How did you know I was here?" Tullah demanded.

"I saw your bag sticking out of Louise's pocket. She tried to plead ignorance at first but I soon got the truth out of her."

"My bag! I dropped it. Louise must have picked it up." She gave a small shiver. "Oh, Saul...I feel so sorry for her. She obviously loves you very much."

"Not any more," Saul assured her dryly. "In fact, I suspect that right now I'm number one on Louise's personal hate list and shall be for a good long time to come. She did at least have the grace to say that she was going to come back for you," he told Tullah soberly, "but my God, when I think... I didn't know whether to shake her or beat her."

He saw the look on Tullah's face and shook his head.

"No, of course not," he acknowledged chidingly. "I would never use violence as a means of deterrent with any child, and in many ways Louise is still very much a child even though she doesn't like being told it."

He paused and, if anything, his voice became even more serious.

"Will you marry me, Tullah?" He reached out, taking hold of her hand and carrying it to his lips as he went down on one knee in front of her, and to her amazement and delight, proceeded to propose to her as though they were indeed an eighteenth-century lady and her gallant.

"Yes," she whispered back softly. "Yes, yes, yes!"

"It isn't just me you'll be taking on," he warned her when they were finally leaving the maze. "There's the children, as well."

"I know," Tullah assured him.

"Which reminds me," Saul added, his eyes gleaming with amusement and something else that made Tullah's heart start to pound a little as he drew her against his side. "Tonight the children are sleeping at Queensmead, which means that we will have the house to ourselves, which means..."

He paused and Tullah prompted, "Which means..."

"Which means," he teased her tenderly, "that you'll have ample opportunity to show me how much of this dream of yours you can actually remember, because I can promise you that I remember every single second of it…every single second…every single kiss…every single touch…every single…"

"Saul," Tullah warned him breathlessly.

EPILOGUE

"WELL, all's well that ends well," Olivia commented to Caspar as they stood on the lawn at Queensmead in the hot August sun and watched Tullah and Saul moving amongst their wedding guests. "Amelia looks so sweet in her bridesmaid's dress, doesn't she?" she remarked fondly, patting her stomach as she added, "She keeps asking me how long it will be before the baby comes out of my tummy."

"Mmm...well, another six months is going to seem an awfully long time to her."

"Jenny said she'd had a letter from Louise earlier in the week. Apparently she's enjoying herself in Italy and working hard. Jenny thinks she's finally getting over her crush on Saul."

"Well, Saul certainly made it plain enough to her that she didn't have a hope in hell of getting any response from him when he found out she had trapped Tullah in the maze," Caspar responded.

"Mmm. I think that was what shocked Louise

to her senses," Olivia agreed. "It's lovely the way Saul's three have taken to Tullah, isn't it?" she asked him, watching with a smile as Jemima positioned herself firmly at Tullah's side. "Especially Jem. She's really starting to come out of her shell under Tullah's influence."

Smiling lovingly down at Jemima as she reached for her hand, Tullah gave it a small reassuring squeeze and leaned against her new husband.

It had been worth all the effort and secret phone calls and appointments she had had to make to see Saul's face when he had turned to her at the altar and he had realised that her wedding gown was virtually a copy of the period costume she had worn the night they had declared their love for one another in the maze.

She had determinedly stuck to the same theme for the whole of the wedding, and as Olivia had ruefully told her judging by the awed eagerness of their local newspaper photographer, their wedding was going to be *the* wedding of Haslewich's summer.

Tullah had simply laughed. She wasn't in the least interested in what other people thought, not really. It had been for Saul that she had endured the tedious fittings and the long discussions over fabrics and patterns, and it had been worth every single second of the time she had spent just to see that look in his eyes in church. The look that was *still* in his eyes right now, she acknowledged as she felt him watching her and turned her head to smile at him.

"Have I told you yet how beautiful you look?" he asked her gruffly.

"Of course you have, Daddy," Jemima answered for him. "You've told her loads and loads of times."

Over her head Saul gave Tullah a rueful look. "Are you *sure* it's a good idea to take the children to Portugal with us?" he asked her, referring to the fact that in the morning all five of them were flying out to that country for a month's holiday. "Some honeymoon you'll have."

Although he was smiling, Tullah knew what was prompting the small shadow she could see at the back of his eyes. She knew because they had already discussed it, or rather Saul had discussed it, asking her how she felt about it one night as she lay happily in his arms, her body aching deliciously from his lovemaking.

"Are you *sure* you don't mind…having the kids

with us when we go to Portugal? It seems unfair on you. It is your honeymoon after all."

"Our honeymoon," Tullah had reminded him firmly. "And yes, I *am* sure. We're going to be a family, Saul, and I want the children to feel as secure in my love as they do in yours. If that means sacrificing the pleasure of being alone with you for the pleasure of knowing that they feel secure and loved, then I know that it's a sacrifice I'm more than willing to make. There'll be plenty of time for us to go away alone together later once the children have accepted my presence in your life, in their lives. It isn't going to change their relationship with you. Yes, of course I'd love us to be able to go away on our own," she had admitted, "but you and I are adults and the children aren't."

"You're a woman in a million, do you know that?" Saul had whispered.

Tullah had smiled a very feminine and knowing smile as she snuggled closer to him. She had no intention of correcting him and telling him that in actual fact she was simply a woman in love, very much in love.

She was remembering that conversation and that night now as she shook her head and told him softly, "Our honeymoon is going to be wonderful, and all the more so because we'll have the children with us," she promised him lovingly, and meant it.

She knew he felt that in being divorced and the father of three children he had deprived her of the right to start their marriage with both of them on an equal footing, both of them "new' to the state of marriage, both of them able to concentrate exclusively on one another, but Tullah, whilst appreciating his feelings, she didn't share them.

She loved the children, she had assured him, for themselves as well as because they were a part of him. Now that she knew him and the circumstances of his first marriage, the fact that it was, as he freely admitted himself, a mistake right from the word go, she no longer had any doubts about his ability to remain faithful to their marriage vows—far from it.

He loved her and he showed it, in oh, so many different ways, in bed and out of it.

As she felt him looking at her, she looked back at him.

"Well, at least we've got tonight," he murmured. "The kids are staying at Olivia's."

"And we've got to be up at eight to pick them

up and catch our flight," Tullah reminded him with a grin, but although she was teasing him she couldn't hide the expression in her eyes from him and she knew that he was well aware that she was looking forward to the evening that lay ahead of them as much as he was…every bit as much as he was. To their whole lives together.